MICHAEL BURGE is an Australian author and journalist who lives at Deepwater on Ngarrabul Country in the New England region of NSW with his husband and their dogs.

His debut novel *Tank Water* and its sequel *Dirt Trap* (MidnightSun Publishing) are a rural noir storytelling cycle exploring homophobia and queer justice in the bush. A gothic mystery *The Watchnight* (Histria Fiction) is a bold re-imagining of the Methodist settlers who colonised Australia's Jenolan Caves in the 1850s. A memoir *Questionable Deeds: Making a stand for equal love* (High Country Books) lifted the lid on familial and institutional homophobia in Australia during the marriage equality campaign.

Michael has written, edited, directed and broadcast for Guardian Australia, Fairfax Media, United News & Media and *The Journal of Australian Studies*. A graduate of Australia's National Institute of Dramatic Art, he is a board member of BAD Sydney Crime Writers Festival and a member of the Australian Crime Writers Association.

His complete works can be found at www.burgewords.com

'I love reading Michael's work. An elegant, flowing pleasure combining journalistic rigour with literary excellence.'

Margo Kingston, journalist and author

'It's time to move beyond a city perspective on rural gay Australians – so often imbued with pity, condescension and silly stereotypes – to hear our own voices on our own terms. Michael Burge is one of our most compelling, nuanced and enjoyable voices.'

Rodney Croome AM, LGBTIQA+ equality advocate

TITLES BY MICHAEL BURGE

Fiction

Dirt Trap

The Watchnight

Tank Water

Closet His Closet Hers

Non-fiction

Questionable Deeds: Making a stand for equal love

Pluck: Exploits of the single-minded

Write, Regardless! A no-nonsense guide to plotting, packaging &
promoting your book

Creating Waves: Critical takes on culture and politics

Plays

Merely Players

For information about upcoming titles go to
www.burgewords.com

CLOSET HIS CLOSET HERS

collected stories

MICHAEL BURGE

'False face must hide what the false heart doth know.'

William Shakespeare, *Macbeth*, Act 1, Scene VII

First published in Australia 2015 by www.burgewords.com
Reprinted 2019

This new edition published in Australia 2021 by High Country Books
An imprint of The Makers Shed www.themakersshed.org
Reprinted 2025

ISBN: 9780645270501

A catalogue record for this book is available from the National Library of Australia

Contents

Last Job of the Day

HOW COULD THE kid be *so damned sure* why Pete was here?

He'd turned off the highway at the park near home, and onto the dirt road which led into a tea tree thicket that ran up the ridge.

He was on his way home, but he had one more very important part of his job to do before he could call it a day.

From the top, past where the road became rocky, Pete could see the railway bridge and the highway.

The train would appear at any moment, glide silently around the bend of the track, then accelerate towards a straight stretch of track with city views.

But he'd noticed the kid at the entrance to the little park, the light of the toilet block outlining the side of a young face mainly hidden beneath a blue hoodie.

By the time Pete had negotiated the rocky section of road, head banging twice on his window, he'd seen that blue hood again, this time in his rear-view mirror as the kid weaved in and out of the tea trees towards him.

A patch of sky tore open the darkness for a moment longer. Pete's throat went dry. The kid was getting closer, in no hurry. Tall. Thin.

A rush of air and Pete's attention was on the sudden train.

Tiny undulations rippled across both tracks, just as they should. The silhouette of the driver appeared and was gone in a moment, and Pete waved. The guy would see the railway logo on the side of Pete's ute and wave back.

Sure enough, he saw a man's arm go up before rusted shipping containers of every colour slid past with the grinding *sweep-snap-sweep-snap*.

Pete looked in his mirror again. The kid was now just metres away. *So damned sure.*

Pete looked at the containers again. Unconsciously, he counted them. The sun dipped lower for its last flush, and between each carriage a flash of light filled his vision, so that he did not see the silhouette arrive at the passenger window, or feel the door open as the kid slid into the front seat.

'Just checking the railway bridge,' Pete said, eyes still full of sun.

'Yeah?' the kid said, fidgeting.

'Last job of the day,' Pete said, nonchalantly, then cleared his throat.

'Yeah?' the kid said again.

'Just have to wait for the train to pass.'

'Okay.'

'Gotta check the bridge,' Pete added.

The containers continued. Pete had lost count, so he started again, and was soon up to thirty, when the kid fidgeted again.

As brightly as a light going on, the last container revealed the boy to the man, and a youthful hand ran across Pete's thigh.

Pete stopped it by grabbing the wrist. The kid's hand instantly relaxed. Both of them exhaled, and the hand found Pete's hardness.

'Door shut?' Pete groaned.

The kid nodded. Pete felt the hooded head brush across his shoulder. A cheek came to rest on his thigh.

Both hands quickly undid him. They knew the way. Pete locked his eyes on the vinyl ceiling of his cab.

It always started so fast.

When he looked at the clock on the dash over the kid's head movements, the little green lights showed it was five thirty-five. By then Pete was too far gone to care. He exploded and shoved his feet against all three pedals at once, letting out the cry of a little bird.

He pushed the kid out the door, wrenched the keys around, reversed roughly into the undergrowth, and accelerated down the rocky road, his head hitting the window as he got away.

At the toilets, he saw the bloke from the general store lock his gaze onto Pete's ute. Pete indicated a left turn, accelerated onto the highway, waved at the bloke to make it seem normal, and was gone.

The clock said five forty-one as he turned into his driveway. His daughter's bike was in the way, but he didn't sit on the horn, Pete moved it himself.

Fresh air revived him in the darkness that wrapped around the house, and the glow from the glass by the front door allowed him to see as he pushed the bike onto the wide porch, pushing it between the family shoes and the coat rack so it would stand up by itself.

Wiping his hands on his pants, he realised his fly was still undone, with a wetness on the zip edge as he flicked it up and shut. He cleaned himself with an oily rag from the tray, and went in for his dinner.

The next morning, he worked on his wife until she screamed out his name. That was the moment he finished her off, never before.

It usually woke Katy, and he would leave their daughter to Trish while he made the tea and toast and put the breakfast things on the table.

This particular morning, he wondered for a moment if he'd hurt his wife. Trish lay gasping as though he'd run her through. They fell apart like warriors after battle, pleasure spilling off the bed as the stirrings came from the kids' room.

Trish pulled her nightie down and went to see.

Pete leaned against the kitchen sink, looking out onto their flat block. The upturned water tank. The dog chained to the old car. The smoke from their back neighbour's chimney.

He wouldn't do it again, he swore. That was it now. He'd tried it enough, and if the bloke from the general store said anything he'd just say he had to check on the bridge. Last job of the day.

THE occupational therapist seemed to have given up on them. She was lingering by the nurses' station. The way she kept looking sideways at them, and the manner in which the nurses laughed straight afterwards, Pete was sure she'd said something.

'How much longer you want to be here love?' Pete asked Trish, who was combing their son's golden hair and pushing it back from his face.

His son was gazing up to into Pete's face. He avoided the blue eyes and looked back at the therapist, who was sipping a coffee now and still making those bloody nurses laugh.

'We haven't had our lunch with Mummy and Daddy yet, have we Billy?' Trish said.

Pete couldn't stand the lunches. His son Billy was eleven and still needed to be fed, needed the coloured mush shoved down his gob with the spills scraped off his cheeks, and Trish was good at it. She scraped every last bit of Billy's slobber into his mouth, and it made Pete gag.

To avoid it, he'd go for a cigarette, which meant he had to walk through the television room to get to the smokers' yard. It took at least half an hour all up, and by the time he got back all the mush was gone and Billy had been wiped clean and was usually ready for his sleep, which is when they left him and drove the three hours home.

Suddenly, a hand pressed against Billy's shoulder. That nurse, the male one. It broke Pete out of the frozen spell he regularly found himself in during these bloody visits.

'Hello Billy,' the nurse said. Billy's eyes lit up and he started thrusting his body this way and that in his frame, the back wheels lifting off the floor.

'Oh he's very excited to see his Mummy and Daddy, isn't he?' the nurse added, settling the child down with strokes on the shoulder.

Billy wouldn't be settled though, he flung his hands at the nurse and they clapped with the fun of the moment, and Billy's freshly combed hair lost its neat part.

The nurse looked at Pete and Trish, one after the other.

'Billy's therapist would like you to stay a bit after lunch. She feels Billy will benefit from a bit more time with you today. It will help when he has his home visit. In two weeks, I think, isn't it? If you spend more time with him now, it will make things easier when he gets home.'

Trish nodded, taking it all in with the same silent smile she always took everything in with.

Pete mumbled in a slightly positive tone, and nodded firmly once.

The nurse nodded back, trying to make them both nod confidently a bit more so that he could tell if they'd agreed or not, then walked off.

Trish fixed Billy's hair. Pete watched the nurse's backside walk tightly to the nurses' station and disappear behind the counter.

Over the next few minutes he watched the guy swing his arms a few times in an animated way, and laugh loudly at someone's joke.

Typical, Pete thought, as the guy put lip balm on an already shiny mouth, then checked his watch.

'I'm going up to the hydrotherapy pool Melissaaaa,' he said, before hitting the corridor with a swagger.

At the last moment, he locked eyes with Pete, who turned away so fast he knocked Billy's trolley with the side of his arm.

'Careful Daddy!' Trish said.

'Alright love,' Pete said.

They wheeled Billy to the lunch room, and since the mush was green today, Pete went for his cigarette before Trish could start any scraping.

There were one or two mums Pete recognised in the tele room, with a few kids in wheelchairs and harnesses, obviously finished with lunch and having that quality time the therapist wanted.

The smoking courtyard was walled on three sides, with the exhaust fans from the kitchen sending a warm funk out onto the headland.

You couldn't see the ocean from here, but you could hear it, just over the noise of the fans and the cries of the seagulls that scavenged in the rubbish skips on the other side of a thick hedge of holly.

There was a plastic bucket filled with sand between two white plastic chairs. Brown scorch marks were melted into both bucket and chairs.

Cigarette butts blew under the hedge and down the grassy ridge.

Pete lit up, dragged in the smoke and blew his first exhalation between pursed lips. *Shit*, he thought, *these trips are a waste of petrol and a day off.*

He only came because Trish had gotten herself lost coming home the first time. Missed the turn off on the freeway and ended up in the city. They hated the city.

They had that in common.

There was only one other father who used to come regularly. Pete had sat with that bloke right here in the smoking courtyard while he'd cried for the better part of an hour about his dying daughter.

That was years ago. Today, the courtyard was empty. There was a smear of tomato sauce down one of the chair backs, so Pete sat in the other one, sucked on his cigarette a few times, crossed his legs and closed his eyes.

The sun on his face made him feel warm all over. He counted how many sounds he could hear. The fans. The gulls. The sea. Something clinking in the kitchen, through the wall. The rush of cars on the road. Doors sliding open every now and then. Feet scuffing, then a voice said: 'Can I scab one of yours?'

Pete opened his eyes. It was the nurse.

'I don't usually smoke, but today's been stressful to say the least.'

'Yeah,' Pete said, sitting himself up and hiding himself behind his arms. He slid the box out from under his sleeve and offered one to the nurse, who fumbled with it, laughed, took two without asking, and laughed again.

When Pete offered the lighter, the nurse pulled the flame and Pete's whole fist closer to his puckered mouth, sucked in hard, then blew smoke over them both.

'I'm on a five-minute special just-so-I-don't-have-a-panic-attack-break,' he said, dragged again, and added: 'Matron knows if she doesn't say yes to one of those, it's the kids who'll suffer more than me.'

Then the nurse laughed. It was as high pitched as the gulls.

'Thanks, though,' he added, indicating the cigarette.

'No problem,' Pete said, eyes on the top of the hedge.

'Billy's a good boy. He's such a good boy,' the nurse said, forcing conversation. 'A little heartbreaker too.'

Pete noticed him cross his legs. 'Everyone loves Billy, and he loves everyone, even the grumpy ones.'

Pete nodded. That would be the case, knowing Billy.

'So how are you coping?' the nurse asked.

'Trish enjoys coming to see Billy,' Pete said. 'I like it when Trish is happy. We go for dinner on the way home. It's better than when we tried to have him at home.'

'You've got other kids. I've seen you before, haven't I?'

'We've got a daughter, and we've got Billy,' Pete said. He was nearly finished his cigarette now, getting ready to make his excuses.

'That would have been hard on all of you,' the nurse nodded, sucking so hard on his cigarette that he was almost finished too.

'We do what we need to do,' Pete said, flicking the butt towards the sand of the bucket, but missing.

For a moment they stood opposite one another. The nurse stopped hanging his head on one side and Pete stopped looking away. *There could be no harm*, Pete thought.

'Thanks for the fag. Feeding my habit,' the nurse laughed, flicking his stub after Pete's.

'No problem,' Pete said. The nurse moved first, showing his backside again, looking to see that yes, indeed, it had been noticed, if not openly appreciated.

Pete stood waiting for a few minutes. Any longer and Trish would be in a mood.

PETE lasted five more weeks before he went to check on the railway bridge again. He'd set up a report about this bridge on his work computer, and he sent it through to the city office at least once before he turned his ute at dusk into the tea tree thicket again.

There was no one around this time. He didn't pause to look at the toilet block, he just ascended the rocky strip, slower this time, and parked on an angle looking at the bridge.

It was a grey day. Everything was flattened under low cloud, and rafts of mist swept in from the direction of the concealed sun. The windscreen was quickly coated by rain. He flicked on the wipers and the radio.

The noise and the dash lights brought him back into himself. For a moment there he'd felt like he was out on the bridge, moving past it, inside a cloud.

Same feeling when you're out front with the ball and no one can get to you, but on the field there's a limit to the space, you can put the ball down in a glorious try, put points on the board and have your back slapped hard.

Out here, at the edge of the town, before the valley dropped down into the limitless grey, Pete needed some crappy song to hold himself together.

Headlights swept on the incoming angle through the thicket. Five twenty-two already. Train any minute. Then what? The other car disappeared away to the right. The song finished, then a city traffic report followed. Pete looked in the rear-view mirror and saw the kid coming up the hill.

He turned to the right and climbed out of sight. The train rounded the corner. Pete strained to see anything in the mirror at the same time as waving to the driver, and once the containers were sliding past, he grabbed his jacket and got out of the car.

Rain spattered on his hood as he flipped it up. The kid wasn't on the road. Pete found a little track going higher into the thicket. It was wetter inside the foliage. Through the green haze he saw the red of the car. To get to it he needed to come out into the open, and he was in florescent yellow.

Then he saw figures, barely moving in the shadows. The kid, with arms around him from behind, another face appearing over his shoulder, younger than Pete but still older than the kid, bottom lip jammed out, jolting.

Pete stumbled forwards, was brushed by two overhanging branches, then held.

Unzipping saw warmth placed into Pete's hand. It swelled up so fast, felt like nothing he'd ever felt, except his own, but this was different. He felt it only from the outside. He smelled it. He ate it. It pressed the back of his throat, as water from the tea tree coursed over his face.

Pete did himself up and was back in his car to see the dash saying five fifty-five.

'WHEN Billy comes home, Daddy...' Katy was whispering in Pete's ear, on his lap, the story book finished and slipping down onto the floor.

'Ye-es,' Pete encouraged, settling her down so she didn't tread all over him.

'When Billy comes home, will he be staying forever and ever?'

'No sweetheart,' Pete said.

'Why?' she asked, starting to play with the cords of his dressing gown.

'Because Billy's so special, he needs a special home just for him, with other kids who are just like him.'

'Do I have a special home too?' she pulled one of the cords tight.

'You have your own room, and your dollies live there with you, right?'

'Yes Daddy, but why can't Billy's special home be here with us, with you and me and Mummy?'

'Because Mummy and Daddy can't take care of Billy properly, remember?'

'Oh yes. That's right.'

Pete moved to pick her up and take her to bed, but she blurted, 'why can't you take care of Billy properly Daddy?'

Pete exhaled. Her little body collapsed onto his and she squeezed him tight.

'Too many questions Miss,' he said, laughing. She was distracted and giggled, and didn't see him wiping his tears on the neck of her flannel nightie.

THERE were drinks at work. Dave was leaving. Promoted, up the line. In two months he'd be working from the city office.

Someone had photocopied a picture of him, enlarged it and stuck it on his locker in the lunch room, and drawn a suit and tie over Dave's huge body.

Someone else had scrawled: 'corporate wanker' across the front of Dave's chest, and someone else wrote: 'Don't forget us when you're on a hundred grand Davo.'

Dave was a good worker, and he had brains too. His wife Leanne sent him on a course five years ago, some management thing with IT on the side, and he'd been going to the gym the whole time, so that none of the booze and hamburgers they all swilled showed anywhere on him.

Dazza, the area manager, ordered in a keg, because no one from out here had ever been promoted that far. When it arrived, a skeleton crew of apprentices was assigned for the rest of the day, and all the boys heeded the call for a piss-up.

Pete was the last one to arrive. He told Trish to stay at home. They couldn't really afford babysitting anyway, and Pete hadn't really gotten on with Dave for a few years.

They'd started at the same time, in the same intake, had ribbed one another at the induction and the training, but Pete was a better maintenance engineer, and got himself into the only regional job for that after three years.

Dave had just shrugged and said he was 'doing the slow burn' with his career, that he just wanted to get off the trackwork and into the office before his body packed it in, because Leanne wanted the boys to go to one of the big private schools in the city.

Leanne and the other mums had decked out the lunch room with streamers and balloons, joined by all their kids off the school bus. There was a barbecue on the verandah, and they took all the chairs out onto the terrace overlooking the railway line and the highway.

There were other wives there for an hour or two. Dazza's Penny and Tezza's Denni, but they took the kids for fish and chips in town before going home.

Dave poured everyone's drinks from the keg, swirling the liquid out of the nozzle like an expert. He'd worked a bar in Brussels when he was a teenager, he announced.

Dazza started it, and they all kept it up: 'You're a wanker,' they shouted at him.

When Leanne and the boys left they watched as Dave walked them to the car.

Someone muttered 'noice arse' and she heard, then gave them all the finger, to much applause and a brown eye from Dazza.

'Little slut,' Dazza muttered, doing himself up. 'I'd like to give her one. She's probably gagging for it,' and slapped Pete on the back.

Pete was pissed, but not as pissed as everyone else. He held himself together by sitting on the edge of the pack, slightly out of sight. He'd had three hamburgers just to feel like he was doing something and joining in.

At nine, the stripper arrived.

'We ordered the wrong one Davo,' Dazza announced, 'either that or they've sent a chick by mistake. Will she do, or do ya want a muscle man?'

'Dazza would be happy to oblige, I'm sure,' someone else yelled.

Dazza flashed his dick regardless, and motioned the woman into the middle of the lunch room. She placed her stereo on the table, placed herself on it too, ripped off her shiny black trench coat and yelled: 'Stand back for Jada of the Jungle!' before she was surrounded by the animals.

Dave was slapped on the back a hundred times, pushed to his knees before Jada while she wrapped her legs around him and threw her blonde hair in his face and neck for a minute.

Pete hung back, half yelling, mouth open for more booze, beetroot stains down the front of his shirt.

A man clapped hold of him from either side and held him up. He slid one hand down the back of Dazza's pants and with the other reached out for the arse of the man in front, one of Davo's mates from school.

Any less booze in them all and Pete would have been fully exposed. As it was, part of him was crying out to them all: *Can't you tell? Can't you?*

THEY were supposed to go for fish and chips at eight, because there was going to be a stripper.

But Nick managed to avoid his mother's searching looks by hiding at the end of the verandah in the half light, watching her hunt for him in the darkness below, and pretending not to hear when she yelled for him, voice not quite loud enough to out shrill the juke box she'd hired for the night.

'He can't get up to anything here,' Dad said to calm her down.

'Well, don't let him see the stripper, that's all I ask,' mum said, then kissed Dad in front of everyone.

A great noise went up between the men as their women extricated themselves from a room which was starting to bristle.

While the men kept drinking, Nick finished a few half empty beers on the balcony and chucked the bottles into the bush, listening to the way they clinked away into the darkness, down the rocks. One even went over the cliff edge. He heard it bounce but not hit the bottom.

He watched his Dad dance the stripper into the room, pick her up under her armpits and plonk her on the table. Based on previous experience, Dad was already past remembering anything.

So no one saw while Nick sat at the side of the crowd of men, downing the dregs of any glass he could see.

One of the men forced his father's head between Jada's legs, where Dad was slipping notes left, right and centre around her white undies. Each note made her cry with faked pleasure, and as the heads of men pushed closer towards her, she held her finger up, admonishing their interest, making them keep their distance.

Then Nick saw the bloke, and what he was doing. He was pissed, shirt ruffled over dirty work pants, and he stood at the back of the group. All of a sudden he slipped his hand down the back of Dazza's pants. Dazza was too pissed to notice, and yanked his pants up, slapping the bloke on the back and encouraging them all to look at Jada.

But the bloke wasn't looking between Jada's legs. He was grabbing the arse of another man. Not so tightly that it would be noticed, but sort of patting it, whipping it a bit, encouragingly. When the men leaned in a group over Jada as she flung her undies over their backs, the bloke pulled this guy's pants open and looked right into his bum crack.

Nick remembered that look. He'd seen it a couple of times before.

Jada covered up, cried: 'Thanks boys!' and was gone, all of them watching Dad carry her to her little green car and wave her off into the night.

Dad came back in, raucous and clothes half off.

'What's the matter Dave?' Dazza hooted, 'why didn't you give her one? Disappointed it wasn't a fella?'

'You'd know Dazza, we all know where to find you on a Friday night, up by the bridge with the poofters,' and Dad laughed, slapping the other man and looking for another drink.

THE first time Nick went to the bridge was a Saturday around midday, and a family was picnicking at the mossy tables up from the toilets. He'd told his Dad he was meeting some school friends at the golf course. Dad thought that was a great idea.

There was nothing about the place, no sense of anything. Nick pissed at the urinal, and checked out the graffiti in the one cubicle that had no door. *Meet me here at midnight on any Saturday* was scrawled across the wall. *Was here on the 16th but no one showed. Leave another message if you're serious,* was written over it in red.

He loitered around the park for twenty minutes. A car slid in from the highway and circled around, from one end of the place to the other. Nick felt it slow down as it passed him, and then he understood.

He couldn't see through the windows. It hovered. He put his head down and kept walking, all the way to the service station.

The next time he went to the bridge he said he was going to Andy's place after school, which was in the same direction. Mum gave him till eight to come home or she'd come looking for him.

Nick walked the length of the park, just like he had before.

A red car came off the highway and drove up towards the bridge. Nick followed. The car slowed at the top, and he walked right up to it.

The window was already down. An arm leant on the door and part of a face showed in the side mirror. Beard. Not too old.

'You want anything?' the man asked. He was dressed in a suit, and turned to look Nick in the eye. 'How old are you?'

Nick turned away and walked off. The car reversed, turned and followed. Nick looked as he passed, and the bearded guy flicked his tongue at Nick, the way those devils did in pictures in his art history classes, and sneered. He started to jog, and ran all the way home by six.

The next time he decided to sit at the gateway and catch glimpses as they came in. It was late on Friday and Andy was the excuse again.

At about five-fifteen a white ute came sliding into the park and turned up towards the bridge. Nick saw who was driving. It was that bloke. He followed, immediately, pulling his blue hood down as he neared the truck. At the last minute a train slid across the bridge.

Nick waited a moment in the pulsating air that came off the train, his hand on the passenger door handle. His mouth went dry when he saw the hairy legs emerging from the bloke's shorts, but he pulled the door open and got in.

A WEEK later, Nick went to the bridge again, got there at five and went up into the tea trees.

A train passed, and that familiar red car with the bearded guy came up the hill, so he pressed himself even deeper into the trees.

It went to the far end of the park and stopped.

Before the sound of the train disappeared from the valley, a cop car slid into the park, pulled up behind a low stand of trees, and turned its lights off.

Minutes later, a van pulled in and went the other way. A guy got out and dawdled around the toilets at the edge of the light. When another car arrived, the guy got in and they drove up the other way.

Nick saw the cops get out of their car, using a torch to cross the shorter distance between lines of trees.

They stopped at the van, wrote down license plates, then shone torches on the other car.

The men got out. One of the cops pointed at them, waved his pen around, shone his torch in their faces, and gave them each a paper.

Nick waited until the cop car left, then walked home the long way around.

DYLAN Radley had it in for Nick. Twice after PE he'd tripped him up on the way into the change rooms in front of most of the girls, and whenever there was a ball he'd throw it right at Nick's head.

'Let's play hit the poofter,' Dylan would announce, and most of the other boys joined in, flicking him across the top of his head with bags, books or anything that came to hand.

'Takes one to know one,' was what Mum had told him to say. That had stopped working at least two years before. Anyway, they were right, he was one, and he knew it now. Only a more few weeks and he'd be going to a new school.

Dylan seemed to know that time was running out to really get the poofter good, and a swimming lesson was the ideal opportunity.

He waited during the endurance swimming test, when they all had to do at least ten laps of the pool, with the teacher down the other end, and ripped Nick's swimmers off him as he turned to go back up the pool.

Nick stopped to see his speedos sailing over his head and land in the barbed wire of the high pool fence. No one apart from Dylan and Nick knew where they were, but that was part of the cruelty. There were other kids swimming down their end, and inevitably Nick's nudity would be discovered by someone.

Two girls swam past and saw a boy holding his hands over his crotch. They stopped and giggled, and passed it on to two more girls who were about to head up the other end. By the time Dylan was back up there the message had gotten through, and someone yelled out: 'show us your arsehole poofter'. It echoed over the surface of the water. Even the tuck shop attendant heard it.

Nick's heart started to race. He calculated the chances of fetching his swimmers, then decided that was impossible. The teacher didn't seem to know anything about it from fifty metres away, so Nick swam to the middle ladder.

He was underwater a moment, the sun sparkling over his lean body. For a minute things seemed so normal and Nick drank in as much serenity as he could manage, before breaking the surface to the sound of a crowd, and a shrill whistle from the teacher, trying to silence the kids who were jeering. Nick plunged upwards, put his hands on the ladder, and streaked for the change room.

There was a wall of sound to cut through, but he did it. All anyone saw was a slight, tall boy, with a patch of fur under each arm and between his legs, sprint like lightning away from them. He slid on the water inside and landed heavily against the wall.

'Dylan Radley, come back here now!' the teacher called, which let Nick know he was being pursued. He locked himself in a cubicle with a stinking floor.

Dylan came after him, other boys panting behind. Above him, clambering impossibly over the side of the cubicle, Dylan unlatched the door to an audience of ten boys, while pretending to pump his groin into Nick's bum.

'Who's next to give the poofter what he wants?' Brian called to the boys, then whacked Nick across the ass so hard that there was a red patch for a week.

Nick got dressed and never went back to that school.

TRISH held Billy's neck and asked Pete to hold his waist until they had him fully in the bath.

'Don't let go until he's hit the bottom,' she pleaded.

Billy was smiling at them, wriggling with the warmth engulfing him, and getting ready to splash, but Pete held his son's hands under the water.

'Pass me the soap love,' Trish said, 'I'll get his hands,' and they did a quick swap.

As Pete went for the soap dish his elbow was smeared with the shit from the side of Billy's legs, and it flicked across the white walls and ran down into the bath again.

'Pete,' she chided, 'not that soap, Billy's special soap, remember?'

Pete hovered a moment, shit dripping down his arm and plopping into the water again.

'On the vanity,' Trish pleaded, 'quick!'

Pete found the large white bottle, dosed out a handful of it, and slopped it into Trish's waiting hands.

'Clean him between his legs please Pete,' she added, going for the boy's face, which had been smeared with brown since he'd had his top pulled over his head.

Pete rubbed his hands together, then ran them along his boy's legs. Billy wriggled and laughed, gurgling because some water had splashed down his gullet.

'Let me lift him,' Trish said. She did, and the water ran from his mouth, 'now clean him, quickly,' she said, indicating all the shit on his bottom and thighs. 'Daddy's going to clean you up now Billy,' she cooed in his ear.

Pete lathered up again, and wiped his boy with long strokes.

'Get in between his legs,' Trish said, turning to check, 'clean him all up Pete, come on.'

So he reached in and gently washed all that he dare not touch, the blue eyes of his boy locking on the father as it was swiftly and thoroughly done.

'Now rinse,' Trish said, 'empty that dirty water and run some clean. Not too hot.'

'Mummy, can I come in?' Katy called from the hallway.

'Stay out Katy!' Trish bellowed, 'push the door shut,' she muttered to Pete, as the new water splashed into the bath and onto the boy's clean skin.

It must have been too cold, because the boy thrust a fist down on his father's arm. Pete recoiled, and Billy did it again, moaning and dragging in enough air to moan again.

It went on, until Billy was cleaned and wiped and padded and clothed and restrained and medicated and put to bed.

Katy was waiting outside the door when Trish and Pete emerged. Neither of her parents noticed her sitting in the shadows as they piloted themselves to bed.

Trish nuzzled him, running her breasts along his arm. He moved away, pretending to be asleep, when really he was wondering what he'd do when the boy was another five years old.

Would he have to clean Billy like that, even then?

THE kid was by the toilet block and waved Pete's ute down the second it arrived.

Pete hardly stopped and had barely a moment to check he was far enough off the highway that he wouldn't be seen.

Before he'd mounted the rocky section of road, the kid was at Pete's neck.

By the time he yanked the handbrake on, the kid was into Pete's pants, pulling him out.

As the five twenty-five train slid past, the kid's head below the level of the dash, Pete waved to the driver, his neck, head and mouth rigid with pleasure.

THE bloke was resting his head against the car seat. Nick could hear his breaths gradually getting easier. Neither of them knew where to put their hands. The bloke's were held awkwardly above Nick's head, so Nick grabbed one and placed it around him, nestling under it while he wiped his mouth with his own hands.

'You want a rag?' the bloke asked.

Nick nodded, and one was proffered from the glovebox.

Nick looked at the bloke's penis, disappearing into his white undies. He patted it.

'Don't,' the bloke said, 'you getting out?'

'I'm going to a new school.'

'Are'ya?'

'Yep.'

'Orright then, have a nice time,' and the bloke shoved him towards the door.

'My name's Nick.'

'Okay then,' the bloke said, starting the engine.

'I know what your name is.'

'Do ya now?'

'You work with my Dad.'

The bloke squinted into the setting sun. Nick opened the door.

No change in the man's face.

Nick slid out. The bloke was still, like he was asleep, yet he drove away.

THEY took Billy back to the coast, but dropped Katy at her grandmother's on the way.

Katy had to sit on her mother's knee all the way to Gran's, because Billy's special seat took up every spare fastening there was.

When they got to Gran's, Pete announced: 'We're not gonna get him out because it'll take us a bloody hour to get him back in.'

So Gran came outside in her dressing gown and sat with Billy in the back seat while Pete and Trish used the loo and ate the breakfast Gran had prepared.

She loved Billy. He reminded her of her late husband, the face and the blonde hair and of course the searing blue eyes.

'You're a wise one, you are Billy. You're the only one who knows what's going on, you are,' she said, as he gurgled and she fed him chocolate drops while she watched out for Trish because Billy wasn't supposed to have them.

She mopped up Billy's choccie spills, steam rising from their mouths as they hooted and sang: 'Happy birthday for all your birthdays I've missed my Billy boy.'

When they left she held Katy at her side, tears in her eyes for the blonde one on his way back to 'where it's best'.

There was just no other solution, Gran could see it in Trish's eyes, poor thing. Her son Pete she never worried for. She patted him on the back as he hugged her goodbye.

'Seeya old girl,' he cooed at her and she brushed him off.

'Who you calling old, kiddo?' She bounced off him because he was so solid. So good.

Billy knew where he was before they crested the headland road. He shook the seat out of its straps and was on his side, head down behind Trish's seat when they pulled up in the car park.

Inside, they got his wheelchair and pushed him up to his bed.

Trish unloaded the bags of nappies and the ventilator and the medications and suddenly felt able to breathe again.

'I'll give him one more feed, then we'll go, eh darl?' she said. Pete nodded and reached for his cigarettes.

Outside, the day was getting hot. He heard voices before he saw the nurse and his friend, but it was too late to turn away.

'Here, I owe you one, or do I owe you two?' the nurse said, offering his open box.

'Don't worry about it,' Pete said, dangling because there was no spare chair.

'I insist,' the nurse said, 'it's always polite to repay the kindness of strangers, isn't that what they say?'

'That's from an old movie,' the other nurse said, a large woman who Pete thought was about to have the chair collapse under her if she wasn't careful.

'You'll have to loan me that one Dot,' the nurse said, 'that one of your videos?'

'Shut up,' Dot said. Pete raised an eyebrow, 'we're always on at one another. You have to watch this one,' she added, indicating the nurse.

'Time you went back. I've got another five minutes, me,' he said, laughing into his cigarette smoke.

'What would I do without you to remind me, *Simon*,' Dot said, stubbing out her cigarette and ambling her way around the hedge.

Simon wiggled his leg and bit his fingernails. Pete stood stock still.

'Billy boy back then?' Simon piped up, eventually.

'Yep,' Pete said before the other man had even finished.

'Your fag's gone out. Here, let me light you up,' Simon said, covering the ground between them in an instant and making a flame.

Pete thrust the other man against him so Simon would feel what was inside his pants. Simon's eyebrows went up. He slipped a wrist easily under the side of Pete's shiny black footy shorts, and pressed a finger into the side of his dick, feeling for its end.

Pete exhaled, letting his head drop back, and closed his eyes.

Simon whispered: '*Yeah, that's right*,' into Pete's ear, brushing him on the side of his face with his chin.

The scent of perfume and sweat went into Pete's nostrils, and the whole drive to the coast, Trish's insistence on stopping for sandwiches, which had stuck to Billy's face in smears, all disappeared with the touch of this man.

'*Now you listen to me*,' Simon said, breath low under the roar of the fans. 'I've had enough of your type to last me three lifetimes. You only want it when you can get it in secret. You've got no bloody idea what it's like to be gay.'

Pete pushed at him, but Simon's grip on his cock tightened.

'*You're not gay, are you?*' Simon hissed, 'but the guy who's sucking you off is. That's the way it is with your lot, isn't it? Two weeks ago you could have had me, right here, but I've had enough, get it?'

Simon's offended footsteps disappeared, and the automated door swished open and shut. Pete vomited his sandwiches into the hedge, face stung by holly spikes, and didn't go back in until his erection was gone.

THE knock on the front door was a quiet one. Pete heard it from the bathroom, but Trish didn't. He opened it and the light shot out all over Nick, trying to retreat inside his hood at the very edge on the threshold.

'What the hell are you doing here?' Pete blurted.

'I've run away,' Nick confessed, 'I've been waiting for you up at the bridge.'

'How the hell did you find out?'

'I told you, I know about you.'

'I've got my kid in here.'

'I know. I've seen her,' Nick looked him in the eye.

That was too much.

'Now wait here, and don't make a sound,' Pete shut the door quietly. The light diminished and the kid zipped up his jacket. It was cold. Mist was closing in across the bare yard. The bloke hadn't even noticed his new T-shirt, stolen from the shop near the city railway station.

Nick heard Pete say: 'Left something at work darl,' and saw him cross to somewhere else.

He'd answered the door in an open dressing gown and striped pyjama pants with no top on. He had hair from his throat to his belly, but Nick smiled when he realised he already knew that, and rested his bag on the pile of kids' shoes by the door.

The door swept open. 'Don't wait up,' Pete called, eyes locked on the kid but mind focussed on the wife.

'You come with me,' he said, gripping Nick by the arm, so hard that the kid went stiff in his pants.

They drove the five minutes to the park. There were two men in the lamplight who came to life when the ute swung around and up the road towards the bridge. Both the bloke and the kid clocked them and rejected them in the same moment.

Up at the bridge, Pete jerked the hand brake on and folded his arms.

'Your Dad know you're here?'

'He'll know I'm gone by now, but not where. They don't care about me.'

'Whatchya come all the way back here for?'

Nick's silence let them take in the obvious. He reached across to his familiar spot at Pete's lap, but Pete slapped his arm away.

'I'll put you on the train, and you're going home,' Pete said.

'I'll be gone in the morning, if you stay with me all night,' Nick whispered.

Nick thought of being enfolded in those arms, of the great hulking body bearing down on him. He wanted to be Jada of the Jungle for this man, who would bow to him like his Dad had to her, across the softness of a motel bedspread.

That thought was in their future, hanging in the air, making them look ahead.

But the bridge lay under a thick mist, not even the tracks glinted.

Pete thought of kissing the kid, the way that Trish always tried to kiss him. She'd be asleep when he got in. She wouldn't know if he'd been gone all night or not.

A light caught Pete's eyes in the rear vision mirror. He drew breath and turned his head.

Down below them there were lights flashing on top of a car. Torch lights bounced inevitably up to the bridge, up the only way out.

Pete turned to Nick, looked him in the eye, about to shove him out the door and drive through the lights back to the freedom of the highway, but when looked backwards again, the torches were closer now, right on his tail.

He needed air, so he pushed through the door and felt the sting of scrub on his bare legs. He should have worn pants. It was cold.

The only way was forward.

If he could jump the fence the torch lights wouldn't touch him anymore.

He cleared the wire, slid down the embankment, scrambled up the oversized gravel he'd ordered five years before, but before he could look back to see how close they were, Pete was hit at full speed by the eight-fifteen passenger train as it accelerated towards the city.

JESSIE WANTED TO paint, but she was going to start another load of laundry first.

The day was sunny enough for line drying, and as she soaked in the warm light that belted through the kitchen window, the phone rang.

She watched it vibrate, counted the fourth and the fifth rings. One more and the call would connect to the answering machine. She'd hear Helen's voice saying they *can't get to the phone right now*, and she could put on the last load of washing and find her paintbrushes.

But she picked up the phone. 'Hello,' the voice said, 'is Jessica there?'

'Yes, it's Jessie speaking.' It was Terry, dammit.

'Can you do a shift for me today?' he said, launching into his shit. Jessie let him speak, picturing the calendar on their kitchen wall, clear of any handwritten scrawl to tell her there was something she had to do more than take another shift.

'You've been to Mrs. Brooks' before?' Terry asked.

'No, I don't think so,' Jessie said.

'She's fairly memorable. Needs help with a shower, and lunch. I've had three carers call in sick today. People are waiting for their showers all over town!'

Jessie could feel the washing machine on spin cycle in the distance. It always shook the house.

'Okay,' she said.

'Great, I'll text you the address. Get there quickly, okay? I'll put it on your timesheet.'

'Is there anything I need to know?' Jessie asked, but he was gone.

Ten minutes later, she'd put another load of clothes on, slipped a dirty green polo shirt over her head, hung out the washing and was driving up the hill.

The address was slightly wrong. She ended up at the neighbour's, where a middle-aged woman pointed Jessie across her front yard. Between two magnolia trees was Mrs. Brooks' side door.

'She won't mind if you go in that way,' the neighbour said, a little white dog at her feet. 'I often pop in there in the afternoon, just in case she needs something. Say hello to her and tell her I'll be over later.'

The magnolias were magnificently in flower, candles of fleshy petals reaching up to glimpses of sun through other bare trees. The neighbour watched Jessie, and gave her a little wave of encouragement towards the entrance in the shadows of the house.

She knocked on the wooden frame, but the door was ajar. Inside was dark and the silence gave way to a fluttering sound, like the sputtering of toy car engine. As her eyes adjusted, Jessie saw she was in a dining room, leading on to a bar. One of those Seventies home fantasies, a sunken lounge showing from between brick pillars.

As she moved into the half light, the fluttering grew louder. On the bar she saw the plastic medication cases and the little generator on the floor, a green hose leading up the hallway and into a room from which light spilled onto the brown shag-pile carpet.

Jessie took two steps and someone said: 'Mind the hose, darlink. Don't tread on it, will you?'

'Mrs. Brooks?

'Yes darlink, come in, but mind the hose, won't you?'

Jessie trod either side of the snaking line, all the way into the light, where a small woman sat among pillows piled up behind her in a great pyramid, the hose leading up the bed to her face.

Mrs. Brooks looked at Jessie for a moment, adjusting her eyesight.

'Belinda is ill today? What's wrong with her?' the old woman asked.

'Oh, I don't know, Mrs. Brooks. They don't tell us,' Jessie replied.

'She's probably taken her daughter to see that specialist. I told her not to do it, but she doesn't listen to what I have to say. The girl has pimples. All girls have pimples, am I right? We don't all have to see specialists about it, do we? We just need to watch how many sweeties we have, am I right?'

'Yes, Mrs. Brooks.'

'Call me Baba, please. What is your name, darlink?'

'Jessie.'

That made Baba frown. She reached for a scrap of paper by her phone, which sat at the edge of the floral bedspread, and wrangled a pair of spectacles.

'They told me your name is Jessica. Jessie is a boy's name, am I wrong?'

'I've been Jessie since I was a kid,' Jessie said.

The old woman tutted. 'Let me see you, come into the light. Take my hand.'

Jessie was compliant. Baba took her hands, one frail and one with a strong grip, and through her glasses looked deep into Jessie's eyes.

The older woman's skin was like tracing paper. Behind thick spectacles, her eyes shot forward with the extreme magnification, pupils darting left and right.

'You're only a girl,' Baba announced. 'Want to see what I look like?' she asked, frail hand dropping away and indicating a large framed photograph on the wall by the door. In it, a vibrant woman smiled. She'd been caught in the middle of laughing, eyes glinting and great sweeps of hair falling about her shoulders. In the background, out of focus, Jessie could make out the bar in the other room, glasses and bottles creating a blur of reflections and shadows behind the woman.

'Hard to believe, no?' Baba said, letting Jessie go and sinking back into the cushions. Jessie didn't answer. She went for the green folder she saw poking out from under a pile of magazines.

'Leave that!' Baba spat. 'Always it's the folder, the *folder!*'

'I need to check your care plan.'

'Forget it! Belinda hasn't looked at that for six months. That man, that Terry, he always gets it out and talks, talks, *talks* about the care plan. I need you to call for some lunch, and go collect it. There's a menu down here. Get me that and forget about the damned care plan!'

'Yes, Mrs. Brooks,' Jessie responded, in the manner she'd been trained to.

'Do I offend you?'

'No Mrs. Brooks.'

'Then why do you call me that, when I have already asked you to call me Baba?'

'Sorry, Baba.'

'The name my grandchildren call me. I allow you to call me that, and straight away it's "Mrs. Brooks" again.'

'Sorry Baba. Where is the menu?'

'Oh here, down here somewhere. Throw that away!' she was pointing to the green folder.

Jessie pushed the folder into the narrow space by the bed. A pile of laminated menus spilled out of the jumble.

'Chinese today,' Baba said, reaching for one, 'and you must choose something for yourself.'

'Oh, I can have my lunch at home.'

'You don't like to eat with me, even when I am paying?'

'Well, we are not supposed–'

'Terry won't find out. What do you want?'

The old woman passed Jessie the menu, slowly turning her shrivelled arm as she pushed the cracked plastic across the gap between them. Jessie saw the red and gold dragons, coiled on either side.

Baba's upturned wrist slid into view, where six numbers were tattooed in an efficient row, slightly raised off the milky whiteness of the taught underarm skin.

As Jessie looked from the numbers into the old woman's face, Baba was nodding. Nodding for her to choose a meal, or nodding to say, *you've seen it, yes?*

Baba withdrew her arm, bringing its weakness back into the protection of her other hand, faded thumb brushing the concealed numbers, as she said: 'I want the black bean sauce.'

'THERE can't be many of them left,' Helen said later that night, as they were wrapped around one another in front of the news. 'She must have been very young, in the concentration camp. Maybe she went there as a child?'

'Maybe,' Jessie said.

'So, do you get that shift every week now?' Helen asked, with a push behind the question.

Jessie stiffened, smiled, and turned to her girlfriend. 'I don't know. It's up to Terry. It's always up to Terry.'

'Have you asked him?' Helen pushed again.

'Not yet,' Jessie answered, wriggling away and going to make the tea. Helen took the rest of the space on the sofa, and as Jessie disappeared into their tiny kitchen, Helen yelled: 'Two sugars darl,' but Jessie was still in the door frame, watching Helen flick the channel over to one of those current affairs shows.

'SHE'S punishing Belinda, for having a day off,' Terry said on the phone the next morning, 'and she's asked for you again ...'

Jessie let out a sigh, was about to speak, then sighed again. 'Belinda's going to hate me,' she said after a moment.

'She'll be relieved, more than anything, to have another day off, I should think ... (put that file on top and get the rest of them out) ... sorry Jessica, we're having some problems here. Can you go again today?'

Jessie scrunched up her mouth, chewed her lip, and said yes.

'TODAY, I need to clean myself,' Baba said, and Jessie nodded. At last, something she knew how to do.

'Don't tangle the hose, will you?' Baba demanded, as Jessie helped her stand by the bed, smelling the fear on the other woman, who guarded her lifeline with her one strong arm.

'Now Baba,' Jessie asked, 'how much help do you need in there?'

'Stay in with me, *darlink*,' Baba breathed heavily as they negotiated their way into the ensuite.

As she lowered the older woman into the waiting plastic chair, Baba clutched at Jessie's arms, only letting go as the warm water coursed over her frame, exhaling with pleasure as she tilted her head back.

'Wonderful,' Baba kept saying, swaying her head under the stream, using all her strength to keep her body upright.

Jessie started on her feet and legs, and Baba allowed her to gently clean down there. At the thighs, the one strong hand wrenched the soap from Jessie's and Baba growled: 'Look away.'

Jessie waited, getting her knees wet, until Baba said: 'Please do the back of my neck and finish with my hair.'

The scents of soap, shampoo and moisturiser revived them from their watery struggle. Jessie held a mirror so that Baba could do her own hair, and the steam and toiletries softened her eyes enough for Jessie to see the real woman for the first time, within the glow of cleanliness and comfort.

After a slower journey back to the bed, after which Jessie ran a hand along the hose line, Baba smiled and said: 'Good girl, my thanks to you,' and rested back into the pillows. 'Belinda has gotten into bad habits with the showers. That was wonderful.'

'Good, Baba.'

'It's ugly to be old, no?'

'Oh ...' Jessie left it hanging.

'Now you're to tell me everything about yourself. We've showered together, so we must know more about each other, to catch up with the intimacy, no?'

'Yes, Baba.'

'You have a ring. What is your husband's name?'

Jessie was prepared for it, and had already looked away, but straight into Baba's eyes in the photo, which were even more searching. The moistness in the air left her, and she swallowed.

'Helen.'

Baba inhaled, was about to speak, but swallowed it.

'I would like a cup of tea and an egg,' she said instead.

Jessie nodded, and followed the hose to the kitchen.

By the time the egg was done there was music coming from Baba's room. Jessie put the meal onto a tray, selected from a stack on a beautiful chiffonier loaded with family photographs. Children. Grandchildren. Husband. Family get-togethers. Baba was the centre of the energy in all of them, drawing everyone to her side, always exhaling with laughter.

The classical music beckoned her back. Baba was upright in bed, leafing through a magazine, and sniffed at the breakfast.

'Perfect, thank you *darlink*,' she said, indicating that Jessie should also sit.

'I have gotten rid of my husband,' Baba announced, between mouthfuls, 'are you shocked?'

Jessie smiled. She'd been thinking about painting when she got home.

'They've taken him away, and now I have this house to myself for the first time ever, but, as luck would have it, I cannot use it as I wish,' and she flicked the green hose.

'My neighbour thinks I am off to the nursing home too,' Baba added, indicating the woman next door with a dismissive wave, 'but I am going to stay as long as I can. I've heard her, talking to my son. She thinks he likes her. Women like him. He's very good looking. Did you see the photographs? Do you think he is good looking?'

'Yes, Baba.'

'But you are *camp*, no?'

'Ye-es ...'

'He must be very good looking, if a *camp* woman thinks he is good looking, no?'

'I suppose so, Baba.'

'Camp is not really the right word, is it? But I cannot think of the right word. The word for a *camp* woman?'

Baba chewed and Jessie span her thumbs around each other.

'You might have told me, before we showered together. But I've decided to like you, you should know. Now tell me what it is you do? None of you girls are really nurses, so what do you do when you're not showering old women?'

'I am an artist,' Jessie said, in the usual tone, positive but not sure.

'I am an artist also,' Baba said, with real delight, 'you see that one behind you? That is one of mine.'

Jessie turned to look at it. A young woman, head to one side in a pale yellow dress. Not looking at the viewer, but over your shoulder. Over hers, a window and a forest.

'My sister,' Baba said, slurping tea.

'It's beautiful,' Jessie said, immediately drawn to the brave tracts of paint that told the story of that face. Much of the rest of the image was hastily sketched, as though the speed was designed to capture some distant impression before it disappeared forever.

'Killed at eighteen. I did it from memory. Ilse was already weak when the train arrived, but I was strong. I carried her body as far as I could. They took her from me, before we went into the showers ...'

When Jessie turned back, Baba was playing with the shells of her egg, moving them around the plate. She was lit from the side, like the girl in the picture, eyes glistening.

'You can have the picture, when I go,' she said, pushing the tray away.

'BUTCH,' Helen blurted from the bathroom, 'didn't you think of saying that?'

Of course, Jessie thought.

'And she's what? German Jew, or Austrian?'

'I didn't ask.'

'So did Terry say if you'd get that shift from now on?'

Helen's tone was wheedling. Jess watched her through the frosted glass of the bathroom door, shirt lifting above her full, round thighs.

'Darl? Did Terry say—'

'No,' Jessie said, interrupting, 'but I'm getting more shifts next month.'

'Fucking straight boy. Can't he just sort it out so that you get the shifts they said you were supposed to get when you started? We're trying to pay a mortgage here ...'

I know, Jessie thought, drifting into the living room.

When Helen caught up with her, she slipped her arms around Jessie's sides and hugged her. 'Jess, my girl,' she whispered, kissing the back of Jessie's neck and swaying her from side to side.

Jessie put her arms over her head and reached for the short hairs on Helen's neck, running her fingers along one of her favourite places.

'All we gotta do is get you regular shifts, and I can take you away for a dirty weekend, can't I?' Helen whispered.

'Yeah,' Jessie said, with the vague hope it could be true.

'SHE'S asked for you again,' Terry mumbled, the sound of filing drawers scraping open in the background.

'What about Belinda?'

'Belinda's a permanent. I can reassign. Mrs. Brooks is going into a nursing home as soon as a place can be found. It would just be temporary. Okay with that?'

'Okay,' Jessie said, 'and–', but he was gone.

Baba was twisted in her sheets with the blind down when Jessie arrived.

'Did you see the television in the garage?' Baba croaked, voice hoarse, wiping her eyes as Jessie filled the room with light.

'No, what's happened?'

'The police left at five and I have not slept. Thought he could steal my television! Hah! Crept in here, after two. I woke. I can hear a *bird land*, in my sleep. I knew there was someone in the house. He trod on the hose, all the way up the hallway, and I pulled this,' she brandished her metal walking stick, still lying across the bed, 'and turned the light on when I could hear him breathing in the doorway, and I screamed at him that I would kill him if he didn't go straight away.'

She was shaking the stick, just like she'd done for the police.

'Dropped the television in the garage. I know who it is. It's one of Belinda's nephews, I am sure of it. He knew exactly where to come, and which door to use, and what to look for. She doesn't have much money, none of them do. Poor people always covet what others have, and I don't have much. If they'd only asked me I would have given it to them. They didn't have to come creeping around a poor old woman's house in the dark. I might have killed him.'

'I should call Terry,' Jessie said, remembering her training.

'Don't bother him, he's a busy man. The police have been. She called them,' Baba said, pointing to the neighbours, 'I didn't want to make a fuss. Worse things have happened in this world. Much worse.'

'A report will need to be made, Baba, that's all.'

'No!' and it was final. 'Now dear, I need some real food. She's been bringing me the most dreadful cups of tea from her *filthy* kitchen. Make me a cup of mine, please. I've spent the night shouting. My voice is gone'. She drew on the oxygen like a suckling child, eyes wide.

With tea inside her, Baba went for the menus. She ordered three kinds of rice, and butter chicken.

They ate in silence, Baba coating the insides of her mouth with every mouthful, the excitement of ordering draining from her face.

'Every day, I taste less and less,' she said, dejected, 'I used to make Indian food. Better than this ... nonsense,' she threw the fork away with a clunk. 'Now, tell me what you paint, Jessica?'

Jessie's face warmed with the attention. 'Just about everything,' she said, 'but not much lately. More when I was young.'

'But you are still a child,' Baba said, patting the bedspread. 'What do you like to paint?'

'Well, it sounds weird, but I paint people on the train, when I go to the city. I like to paint them when they don't realise I am looking at them.'

Baba leant back with a long sigh: 'Ah, yes. Candid. Mysterious. The real person, no?'

'Yes.'

'And you have not done this for many years. You have given it up because you have lost your faith. You have become a woman and you have no confidence in yourself. You have married, or at least given yourself to someone. To this ... *Helen*, and she does not understand that an artist needs to find herself.'

'Yes,' Jessie whispered.

'That was how it went with me and my first husband. Hermann thought he knew everything there was to know about me, until I gave him the slip in Paris. The look on his face,' Baba said, laughing, 'when I came back to get my Mother's photographs! Like a rabbit who thinks it's a fox. He avoided the camps. Never understood them. He found another woman,' she shrugged, dismissing the vision of the man forming in Jessie's mind.

'Tell me, do you ever think of taking a man? Don't you ever have any *normal* feelings?'

Jessie stiffened. She realised her mouth was open, drinking in what Baba had been saying. Now everything was washing out of her again.

'I'll clean up,' she said. She left without saying goodbye. There was nothing in the care plan that said she had to.

'HOW many shifts am I going to get, Terry? I want you to tell me now and I am going to write them into my diary,' Jessie said to him across the desk.

'Um ... let me look, Jessica. You've been a casual for how long?' Terry said, fumbling.

'Six months. I trained with Belinda, and she got regular shifts after three.'

'Right ...' he trailed off, flicking a pen on the edge of the desk between them. 'Let me have a quick chat to Barb. Help yourself to a coffee and a bikkie,' he said, disappearing.

The office sported yellow walls with bright blue trim around the doors, desperate little attempts at nicety in a building squeezed between a funeral home and a brothel by the railway station.

Jessie walked between the tiny offices. One woman on the phone gave her a wave with her little finger, and a younger woman on the computer in the room near the kitchenette gave Jessie a guilty, then a haughty look, before getting back to the pretence of being busy.

The coffee was instant, a tin of it as large as the urn, which had been steaming away unnoticed since lunch. The mugs were yellow with blue flowers. Blue and yellow was the theme of the whole place, denied by the brown brick of the main wall. Jessie made a cup of tea, bags so weak that the milk turned the whole thing hot and pale.

Outside, there was a smokers' spot in the stairwell. Jessie's arrival sent the pigeons flapping up to where one of the sex workers was emptying the bins into a skip. She was beautiful. Asian. She waved at Jessie after swearing at herself for missing the bin with a big white plastic bag. Jessie waved back.

'Thought you might be out here,' Terry announced, bringing a file under one arm. Jessie offered him a cigarette. He held his hand up like a stop sign, but his eyes went into the pack and had them counted in an instant. He licked his lips and looked at her.

'I'll get straight to the point,' he said, 'it's good in a sense that we're out here, because I can be candid with you. I took your case up with Barb,' he flicked his hand over his balding head, sweeping the strands of hair back in place, 'and we talked about you, at length.'

Jessie dragged on her cigarette, looking away. She knew the tone.

She'd heard it ever since high school, from teachers; from Dad, from Mum, from her older brother; from the matron of the training hospital she left after only a month; from the woman at the dole office; from the TAFE college counsellor; from the boss at the gas company she spent eight months with; from the crew leader on the roadwork stint she worked at for over a year; and now it was coming from Terry.

'You know we've been planning to move into more basic client care, transport to and from the shops, or a doctor's appointment, or just meal preparation and socialisation, etcetera?'

She nodded, watching the brothel windows. The Asian woman was cleaning the inside with a tin of spray and a pink cloth.

'Well, we feel that you'd be more suited to that kind of work than anything else. Barb looked up your training records, and she saw that you scored the highest in those learning modules. You're obviously good at it, so if you were willing to wait until we've landed some clients in that area, then you'd be the first one we'd be calling up to work.'

He almost convinced himself, and she gave him the moment,

gave him hope that she'd say yes, while she stubbed out her cigarette on the brown tiles at their feet.

Then she looked at him, the same look that had labelled her as 'vacant' by people in a similar position to Terry, but was just the face of a woman who knew a job had, yet again, been taken from her.

Thinking she didn't understand, he continued, pitching his voice lower, and speaking slowly.

'There is some concern about your suitability for personal care with some of our clients. The showering. The dressing. You know what I mean. Most of our clients are women, elderly women of a certain generation. For them, to be helped to shower is an act of great intimacy, you learned that in your training?'

Jessie nodded.

'What about your male clients?' she said.

'Well,' he said, offended, 'we hope to be getting more later in the year, but right now, in your area, there are only female clients available for our casuals. I'll send Belinda to see to Mrs Brooks tomorrow.'

'Okay Terry,' Jessie surrendered, 'catch you ...'

'She's off to a nursing home soon, so no doubt Belinda will be keen to wish her well on her way,' Terry said to her back.

But Jessie was already gone. He watched her go, then caught sight of the Asian girl, now trying to clean the outside of the windows, and just making them worse, in his opinion.

JESSIE unconsciously fingered the corners of the new pad of paper she'd bought at the art shop on the way from the office to the railway station.

Inside the first leaf was her sketch of three women sitting at the other end of the carriage on the journey home. Jessie still had the marks of the ochre pastels on her fingertips, and on the edges of her pants pocket.

When Helen got home last night, dinner wasn't on and Jess was clearing the garage. She'd unpacked all her boxes that had been under the house ever since she'd been living by herself last year.

She knew Helen would be cross but not able to show it, and she knew if she rustled up cheese on toast, Helen would relax with a beer in front of the news and ask no questions, and Jessie had been right.

The morning sun filled one end of the garage with warm potential.

The washing machine was on spin, and would be finished in a few minutes, then Jessie would hang the clothes out and get to Baba's by nine.

For now, she breathed evenly in the dusty light, rubbing her hand down the door frame. Helen had showered and gone long before.

They'd smiled and kissed on the threshold, and Helen had forgotten to check if the neighbours were watching.

'TERRY told me Belinda is coming back today, darlink,' Baba said, lifting herself against the pillows, a little confused at seeing Jessie so early.

'He must have made a mistake,' Jessie said, wrangling the oxygen hose.

'Always making mistakes,' Baba tutted.

Jessie pulled a face and nodded in agreement.

'At least you're early. My son is coming today,' Baba announced. 'I want to shower, because he hates smells in the house,' she added, reaching for Jessie's arm and launching herself upward.

As she did, Baba noticed the smudges of ochre on Jessie's hand.

With her angular thumb, Baba drew the last of the pigment across the taught skin of Jessie's palm, looked into the younger woman's eyes, and emitted a low chuckle that began as a tremble deep in her frail trunk.

'Ah-ha, it begins,' Baba said, wagging a finger, her face stretching into a smile.

And so, they started their silent water dance.

'Belinda will be back on Monday,' Jessie assured, as Baba covered herself from neck to knee with towels. Three days ago she'd only covered her waist.

'I'll be long gone,' Baba said, lifting her shoulders impishly as the water started to course over her.

Jessie watched her in the reflection of the mirror, but as the steam rose it made Baba disappear.

It was not an unfitting transition, but Jessie needed more.

As she helped with Baba's feet, she noted the shapes of the toes, the kinks that gravity had worn into the old woman, and the way her bones still allowed a waist and bust of sorts, but only the barest of both.

As she helped Baba dry her face and hair, Jessie was drinking in composition and form: the Teutonic facial structure, the signs of deep betrayal in the jawline, the traces of pain around the eyes, the pride still visible in the nose, and the coquettish locks of hair, some still black as night, others faded like the last of a summer's day, soft as haze.

Jessie held the mirror, but knelt on the floor so that she could catch the head from another angle, a portraiture technique she'd teach one day, but didn't realise in that moment.

'Do my hands, child,' Baba whispered, shaking one flexible limb towards the bottle of moisturiser.

Jessie clasped the old woman's hands between hers, the balm soothing them both.

It was cold, and Baba giggled at the sensation, which quickly gave way to warmth. Jessie worked their fingers together, dragging them back and forward, the whiteness of the balm disappearing until there was nothing between them.

Baba's head rested on the back of the chair, a rolled white towel supporting her neck, her jaw dropped in deep relaxation.

Jessie turned their hands over to rest palms up in the light. Without thinking, she wiped a dollop of moisturiser that had escaped on Baba's upper arm, and slid it across the tattooed numbers.

Baba didn't flinch.

'Helen told me there were lesbians taken to Auschwitz too,' Jessie whispered.

'I know, *darlink*,' Baba said softly, 'but we didn't talk to them. They did all the worst jobs.'

AND I AM back, just as quickly as I was when they put me under to sew up my wrists.

There's the nurse, smiling at me from where the tubes run up. She says, *you'll probably feel a bit sore,* then smiles again and writes some notes.

She's only writing down the numbers that appear on the machines. I could do her job, it's just meet-and-greet. They should have people like me doing this kind of work.

The naturally confident people-person type, *here in between the theatre and the real ward,* I say.

I laugh out loud and it sends pain deep inside. I am used to pain, after the dreadful life I've lived, and she smiles again and nods without looking.

Have I gone back to thinking half of what I am supposed to be saying?

I have, but they probably hear all kinds of shit coming out of the mouths of the recently butchered.

I want to feel down there, so I wake one of my hands and reach for the dressing where they warned me there'd be swelling, but I stop.

What if I still find him there?

So I imagine this is the morning after the night before and I've taken something else on top of a few drinks. The numbness could almost be the same. The pain's on hold.

But the waiver makes me waver, I hear myself saying. The nurse doesn't flinch. She didn't hear me saying it to the surgeon in his office, when he laughed at me.

There are some risk factors, but they are negligible, he said.

I couldn't help myself, so I replied: *Way too much information, doctor.*

He smiled a very sweet smile, the kind of smile that tells you you're being convincing on the surface.

But I've always been unlucky. If anyone was going to fall into the one per cent it would be me. That's probably why the nurse is forcing that smile – they've got it wrong and they'll have to do it again. Or they can't do it at all and he will always be here.

Don't say it out loud. I can't live with him. I tried, but I can't.

Those large silver bracelets I got in Bali, I say. It just slipped out. I used to wear them whenever I went anywhere near a medical type, because they were enough to cover how much I can't live with him. When I cut myself I used a name the psychologists would never find even if they tried, the silliest name I have ever used.

My scars are exposed so I pull both hands up. One is connected to tubes, and I laugh because it's like a puppet on a string, that one arm, while the other is free and I want to cry since it's always been like that, always this bit can go that way but not the other, because he was always there.

The useless weight of him, sweat making him uncomfortable even on cold nights. The constant rearrangement as we tossed and turned in bed; and when he needed to piss, God, the pressure. The man who wakes with a full bladder is not to be reckoned with. It's why most men want to fuck in the morning, because they're too lazy to get out of bed.

The nurse looks. She won't be up on the ward, this one; these are the nurses you don't ever see again.

I have got to stop taunting people. The only one I should put pressure on is myself.

I draw my free hand down, and immediately the sheet crumples, like a signal to stop, but my counsellor has made me practice overcoming perceived obstacles, and a crumpled sheet just does not count as an obstacle.

I feel him suddenly, resting against my inner thigh, but it is only the idea of itching when you hear a mosquito, not a real bite.

I am swollen and thoroughly bandaged down there, and *my legs have fallen numbly open*.

Did I say that?

I should have been a writer. Okay, I'll approach myself like a writer.

My fingers walk up the hill of my swollen belly, and in the new country beyond the crest, they discover nothing. Not a rock, stone, tree or branch.

Only the strong, sure sign that there is now a cave below in the ravaged fold, and he is long gone.

Dirty Nurse

MARILYN GOT THROUGH her childhood as quickly as she possibly could.

She mastered puberty by filling out her plain school uniform before she was a teenager, and inhabited the body of a middle-aged, overweight woman by the time she reached her twenty-first birthday.

Swapping school plaids for sterile nurses' uniforms only meant Marilyn had more room to fill.

She maintained her weighty hourglass beneath a cotton waist belt, her figure diminished by the enormous regulation veils she starched religiously and spent more time on than the other girls and their hours of makeup.

Marilyn sterilised equipment twice as long as the other trainees, and never scowled when rostered on for back-to-back 'Dirty Nurse'.

It was during one such marathon that Matron noted the size of Marilyn's stout red hands as she carved paths of cleanliness throughout the wards.

Both women had been trained to polarise cleanliness and dirtiness. Matron simply recognised a sterile girl when she saw one, and knew she had little to teach Marilyn when it came to the simple rules of cleaning up after life's messes, and doing it without fuss. Not with a minimum of fuss, but with absolutely none.

Even past twenty-one, Marilyn slept in the damp room at the end of the verandah in her parents' house. Because it was only a five-minute walk from the hospital, she thought it unnecessary to pack her things and live in the new brick nurses' quarters at the top of the hill, where there were always youths smoking against the end wall. They watched for signs of women returning home along the lit pathway from the main wards to the bright, stylishly designed flats, and Marilyn reported such loitering men every time she saw them.

Her parents were almost old enough to be her grandparents. Marilyn was a late, only child and it was the one thing Mum was really concerned about, although nursing proved a rather unexpected safety net to such worries.

Marilyn thrived on night duty. Home was down a quiet lane away from the main road out of town, where a stand of cypress insulated the crusted weatherboard house against the noise of trucks and the nearby school.

In under a week, she mastered the task of sleeping during the day.

Mum would have a mug of hot soup ready when Marilyn returned from work in the morning, and, by nine o'clock, when the world was on its way to school or work, Marilyn was already dozing underneath her satin-covered eiderdown, a small radiator element burning with a constant buzz only feet from her head, which she liked to be kept hot while she slept.

At three, she would wake naturally, turn sleepily away from the radiator to face the fading pony wallpaper, and have another half an hour of rest, rubbing her socked feet together under the sheets.

By five, she sat with Dad beside the fire and he told her the news of the day from his paper while Mum made their only significant meal.

The portions were small. Mum had kept them that way ever since she'd heard the other mothers making 'fat-girl' comments.

That was over a decade ago now, but the stringent portions had only shed weight off Mum and Dad, leaving Marilyn expanding into her uniforms and tracksuit pants, a mystery that Mum never solved.

Mum and Dad watched the news at seven and by eight were in bed. Marilyn was already helping both of them to walk, so that work, for her, really started at seven-thirty, getting her parents cleaned and their teeth brushed with a happy banter she used with older patients on the seniors' ward up the road.

At five past eight, alone at the kitchen table, Marilyn would bite her nails and carve thin slices of cheese off the block Mum stashed in the fridge. If Mum asked about the disappearing cheese, or the missing leftover meat, or the squares of chocolate gone from the old butter tub in the bottom of the fridge, Marilyn had excuses which she swapped and changed to keep her mother off the track.

'Maggie was hungry' was usually enough to convince Mum. The little dog, on her last legs for years now, often scored titbits from all three of them.

The best excuse, however, were the Bethany kids who lived over the back fence. Marilyn often pretended she'd taken them a comfort hamper because she'd 'spied a little one looking hungrily through the wire'.

Mum once mentioned these comfort hampers to Mrs Bethany when both women found themselves hanging clothes on the Hills Hoist on the same sunny morning. The questioning look on the younger woman's face was so obtuse that Mum misread it for stupidity, and meant to tell Marilyn about it later on, but promptly forgot.

After eight-thirty, Marilyn watched television with the volume turned down so low that she learned to lipread without even knowing it. She especially loved game shows, and she would laugh out loud when any contestant or celebrity made smart comments and put down anyone being facetious or unpleasant. Marilyn would ape them at work whenever she had difficult patients and uncouth family members. The attitude, combined with the uniform, created an aura of unarguable authority around her.

At ten, Marilyn would bathe, filling the tiny bathroom with steam so heavy that she never saw her naked body fill the tiny mirror. She liked the water hot, and had permanent red scalds on her hips and arms from easing herself into the clear lava of her nightly bath.

The unveiling of her flesh was a physical pleasure she didn't know how to enjoy. The brush of a towel across a nipple was a genuine pain. The lick of soap between legs was acknowledged like the unwelcome blade of a knife which slips when you're chopping vegetables.

At ten-thirty, Marilyn corseted herself into a fresh uniform, listened for the breathing of both parents in the darkness by their door, locked the house from the cold verandah and strode up the road for an eleven o'clock start. If there were youths against the wall of the nurses' quarters, she would acknowledge them by name.

'Good evening, Nigel Parry,' or, 'I can see you, Michael Bridgeman.' She took their sniggers as a sign of their pathetic caught-out embarrassment.

On the ward, Marilyn placed her black leather bag beside a cold upright locker, hung her bright red woollen cape on a hanger inside it, and scrubbed her hands in the hallway. She had already shamed the evening girls into such accurate handover reports that she need not even speak with them.

Simply looking at the duty list and the immature handwriting, which listed medications given and vital signs taken, was enough to bring a slow wince to her face.

An inspection of sleeping patients would take at least ninety minutes, more if there were corrections to be made to charts or a post-operative patient to check on.

Marilyn had no compunction in reaching out and closing a waking patient's eyes with one hand as she lifted their stomach dressing with another to check for bleeding. Her face was taut with such silence as she did so, that the patients – fear mixed with anaesthetic – found it easier to say nothing while the nurse asserted herself on their bodies.

In the corridors, Marilyn refused conversation unless it was in response to a doctor's request. If Matron asked for updates on an overnight car accident victim or other deaths to report to family members, Marilyn had a special file for these which she would place on Matron's desk around six in the morning so that a meeting with the senior woman was guaranteed after Marilyn finished at seven. Those little meetings were the highlight of her day, and she did all she could to manage them.

She would greet Matron with a smile, not broad enough to suggest an easy night shift had just passed, but with enough flair to be considered a 'trouper' or a 'stick'. Matron would usually offer Marilyn a coffee, brought by another nurse, quite often one who'd trained with Marilyn, now forced to see how much Matron favoured the hardworking and the devoted.

Matron was a paragon of duty, yet nothing baffled her more than the size of this excellent twenty-five-year-old nurse. If the weight got any worse she would say something. Other girls always scored a biscuit at a meeting with Matron, but never Marilyn.

If someone had died, Marilyn had invariably gone to school with them or someone they knew, or went to church with their cousin or 'knew the family', something Matron could not, since she was appointed from the larger hospital on the fringe of the city half a day's drive away. It was Marilyn's mission to make her a local at these regular morning meetings, which usually saw Marilyn home as late as eight or even eight-thirty, with something to tell Mum and Dad about. Dad would say he was sure his daughter would 'have the great woman's job one day, so the old battle-axe better look out!'

This routine went on long enough for the girls Marilyn trained with to drift off into sporadic maternity leave, which knocked many of them off the rosters and out of the flats, sometimes with more than a hint of scandal associated with one of the youths who gradually became ruddy-faced men.

The flats very quickly looked much less modish than they had been. The bricks suffered stains from the flat concrete roof and the creosote on the eaves, and eventually one half of the building was earmarked for demolition when 'funds could be found'.

BY the time Marilyn had her own office, it was much like her bedroom – isolated at the end of a verandah and damp, since Maintenance never finished the guttering.

The office was a reward for attaining the position of Night

Supervisor by the age of thirty, the youngest promotion of its kind in the hospital's history.

There was no new uniform to expand into, only a chrome-plated badge which Marilyn ordered from the town jeweller and collected on her day off.

She was unprepared for the grizzly smile of the young man she'd been a year ahead of in school, who looked at her through the smoky glass of a recent refurbishment.

It was an unusual look which Marilyn did not recognise, and read as a slight retardation.

He fetched her badge, which had been sent away for engraving, and proudly held it up for Marilyn in his gloved hand. She checked the spelling, retrieved her purse, and curtly said: 'Yes please' to the plush velvet drawstring bag he proffered with his other hand.

'You've done well,' he said, 'out of everyone we went to school with, you've done the best,' he added, sniffing at the last minute, signalling that he didn't much like taking on the family business that had been in town for sixty years.

Marilyn thought of something to say, but stifled it, then another thought popped into her head, and she left that alone too, game show-type retorts which she'd never used anywhere other than the hospital. All she could get out was: 'Thank you, Brian Ward,' as though naming him would thwart his unwelcome familiarity.

As she walked away he wondered how much arse any woman had a right to. Still, he thought, she's more of a looker than Lynne. Lynne was his now ex-wife and the mother of their two children, who'd left for the city last weekend.

Mum had told Marilyn all about it, and she'd had it from Merle at the Bowling Club. Merle was Brian Ward's godmother.

Driving home, Marilyn remembered what Brian's look reminded her of. She put it right out of her mind, until at five past eight that evening it came back to her: the face of Pam Cooper, maybe ten years before, in the storeroom where they kept the cylinders of laughing gas.

While running her bath, Marilyn revived the tinny smell of the tanks as Pam handed them to her, only Pam was always slightly careless and had dropped one. It had fallen against a shelf, which twisted the tap and shot a spray of laughing gas over both of them.

Pam broke into giggles first, in disbelief more than anything. She'd fallen to her knees, knew to turn the tap off, but hadn't quite managed. Marilyn had tutted, put her tanks down, and went to help. By the time she turned to Pam the other woman was collapsed over a pile of sterile linen, gripped with silent mirth.

Marilyn hadn't meant to giggle too, but the gas dragged it out of her. She shook her head, trying to be free of it, but Pam slapped both hands onto Marilyn's leg in an innocent, jaunty motion which Marilyn recalled like a bolt of lightning running through a feather.

The two women fell about for only a minute, but in that minute Marilyn was touched more than she'd ever been in her entire childhood.

As Pam gathered her wits and stood, Marilyn saw her breasts in the shadow of her collar, right through the join of her bra to the top of her stomach.

The sight haunted her now, as she slid into the bath.

Pam had three kids to a real estate agent. They'd visited because Mum had it from Coral at cards that Pam was 'going to leave That

Man', and Marilyn had told Mum to tell Coral to tell Pam she was 'welcome anytime with the kiddies.'

Marilyn had to stop the kids dipping their bikkies in their tea. She'd told them it was 'bad for their toothie-pegs', but they still did it. She'd held the little girl and Dad and Mum had a boy each on their knees, but the little lady didn't like Marilyn's broad, hard lap.

Pam hadn't worked since leaving the ward. She'd swapped starched uniforms for an array of stylish polyester outfits purchased during the abundant early years of her marriage.

Marilyn couldn't get to the wedding because she'd made sure she was rostered on for a double shift to avoid seeing Pam walking down the aisle with That Man.

Around their dinner table, Marilyn waited for news of when Pam was leaving him, but the slightest mention of 'things' brought a tear to Pam's eye, and before Marilyn could go for a hug Mum jumped up with one of her 'don't you worry now love' consolations and Dad had taken the boys out the back to the shed. Marilyn was left to watch the little girl, who insisted on pulling at Marilyn's shoelaces, the way Maggie had when she was a puppy.

Only Maggie was long dead. Mum hadn't even given a cuddle or a kiss when they put the little dog in the ground inside an old floral pillowslip.

Marilyn had nearly slapped Mum for taking away that chance to hug Pam. Her hands had been so close to both women, but nobody wanted them. Not even the little girl had wanted them.

That was years ago now. Pam hadn't left That Man. Marilyn sometimes saw the station wagon parked at the supermarket, and caught glimpses of Pam between the aisles, but her jealousy over that stolen hug always prevented her from saying hello.

So Marilyn slid her head into the searing heat of the bathwater, peeling off the memories she was sure would dissipate in the chilled air long before she surfaced.

SHE was elected to the board of the new nursing home units being developed at the hospital. There was a fundraising ball which she avoided by pretending her mother was unwell, and when the paperwork included mention of That Man, now a fully fledged property developer, Marilyn ensured his submission never saw its way to any meetings.

Funds were raised in excess of budget projections, enough to see the old nurses' quarters demolished after years of languishing as storerooms once the provision of trainee accommodation was no longer required.

This allowed the extension of the planned nursing home to include the state's first independent living units, each with its own garden, fronting onto the main road into town so that the oldies had no need to bother anyone to come and go, but someone was always there 'if they got into any strife.'

Matron's last function was turning the first sod as construction started on a stunning autumn morning. By the time the official photograph was displayed in the outpatient waiting room, Matron had departed for her Fijian holiday, two weeks of 'Sun, Surf and Sand!' booked through the local travel agency, the first year the town ever had one.

Marilyn snorted at the application forms which had been left on her desk, and dropped them with That Man's development proposal behind her filing cabinet.

The Recruitment Officer, a new position filled by a thin man in an office next to the Matron's, was simply not up-to-speed with the running of this hospital.

As she predicted, there were no applications for the job, and, in due course Marilyn was offered it by the board. Her only request (even though she'd been offered none) was that the Matron's office be repainted.

She was sent a colour chart, and since she refused to respond to it, the walls ended up a mustardy colour left over when the Recruitment Office was adapted from an old private room the year before.

Her name appeared on the door in neat black letters.

She never took the time to notice that her old office, immediately upon her vacating it, became a storeroom which Maintenance earmarked as 'damp'.

Within Marilyn's first year as Matron, the nursing home was completed, nursing training was phased out and replaced by university courses in the city; the maternity ward was under threat of closure as a result of the Area Health Service's creation by the state government; and Pam had applied for a job on the wards.

Dad had a lot to say about the Area Health Service. Marilyn let him rave on about it, and all the politicians on the news, even though he often forgot the Premier wasn't Neville Wran now, because Dad got angry if you corrected him.

Marilyn fingered Pam's application. There was a passport photograph on it. She had aged, but was still the girl with the laughing gas. Marilyn insisted on interviewing all applicants, despite the Recruitment Office sending around a memorandum that this wasn't necessary.

Pam looked better in person, shook Marilyn's hand vigorously, complimented her on the promotion, and admired the old Matron's indoor plants. She wore a nice scent.

They caught up on news, and Marilyn let Pam tell her about her divorce and the custody battle even though Mum had it from Mavis at the Women's Club, who'd had it from That Man's mother, that he only wanted one of the boys but ended up losing custody of all three of them to Pam.

Marilyn made sure to smile at the up-to-date school photos. The boys looked like That Man but the little girl was Pam all over. Their teeth were good, but that must be the fluoride in the town water more than any warnings about bikkie dipping.

Marilyn told Pam there was a job going as long as she was willing to start tomorrow as a casual, including night duty. She must have been desperate, because Pam accepted on the spot, which meant Pam's mother from the city had disinherited her again and was not paying for any private school fees for the middle boy.

When Marilyn stood to call for a coffee, Pam hugged her suddenly.

'It's been hard,' Pam said breathily.

Marilyn's instant reaction was to push away, but her face was smothered in that scent, and all she could do was pat her flat hands against Pam's arms while unconsciously looking inside the other woman's handbag which had collapsed open on the chair, a few overdue bills on display.

Marilyn's bath time was now eight o'clock. With no more night duty, arrangements had changed somewhat. Mum and Dad now watched the seven o'clock news in bed, meaning that the house was quiet by seven-thirty.

That night, with the scent imagined in her nostrils, Marilyn pulled Pam to her again so that the other woman's body pressed against her breasts. In truth Marilyn imagined Pam relied on the breadth of her bust.

More than That Man could offer was Marilyn's breathy mantra as she touched herself.

Before any pleasure could emerge, she stopped, sat up in the bath, and tutted as she saw water dripping onto the floor.

THE first Strange Fellow arrived in Emergency about six months later. He'd walked in, apparently, from the railway station, looking more like a sweaty wino than someone who was sick. Marilyn read the report of the Night Supervisor, a very young woman from interstate, and tried to decipher the shocking handwriting. There was no diagnosis recorded, and no report from the attending doctor. It was highly irregular.

Three days later the young man checked himself out and simply disappeared.

Marilyn wasn't aware of the pattern until Dad mentioned something he'd seen on the television. She listened to him this once because he'd said a word with such animation that it echoed around the small kitchen. 'Homo-sex-you-alitee,' he said. 'Why they even bother to talk about it I don't know.'

Mum chimed in that Sonya from the CWA had it from Beryl in

the high school office that one of the teachers was a 'well known *homo-sex-you-al*' and no one knew what to do about it.

The next day Marilyn looked through the files and found there had been five Strange Fellows admitted within the last few months.

Two of them had died on the ward and three had been released, undiagnosed, within a week. She'd seen at least three of them. She'd helped to lay out the body of one, and tried to contact his family in the absence of any details in his personal belongings. The matter had been referred to the local police to resolve and Marilyn had never heard the outcome.

There was also a brochure, which she had to fish out from behind her filing cabinet. On the front was a man riding a horse, his face a skull, and he carried a scythe. On the top it read 'The FACTS – AIDS is God's way of ridding the world of Homosexuals'. It had been left under her office door, like many things were, overnight.

There were quotes from the Bible. Even though she hadn't been to church since Dad stopped going in 1970, Marilyn remembered some of the words, and the angry face of the Minister, a man that Mum loved as much as she loved Dad, if you believed everything she said about him.

Marilyn left the brochure in the bin outside her door where it could be seen, and wrote to the Area Health Service for more information.

Before she got a reply, eight more Strange Fellows were admitted. She heard two university nurses gossiping about it in the new staff lunch courtyard (created when her old office was demolished). She told the girls off. One of them had the gall to say: 'But they're infectious,' before Marilyn calmly told the girl to come and see her at the end of her shift.

The girl never turned up. The Recruitment Office sent a memorandum informing Marilyn that she had resigned.

The next morning, Marilyn attended the doctors on their rounds, politely replacing the ward nurse by asking her to 'special' Mrs. Dillinger while the old lady started what was to be her last day.

Doctor Devine nodded to her and matter-of-factly went about his business in the way Marilyn had trained all the doctors to communicate with her nurses.

One of the Strange Fellows was in the third room, the curtains drawn around him on all sides. Devine lowered his tone while he checked the man's vitals, and inspected a large purple lesion on his neck. The man was in obvious pain. Devine did not cope well with obvious pain. He usually managed a smile if there was hidden pain, one of those disarming, Mediterranean smiles which made everyone else smile too.

But not today. He muttered about an increase in morphine, monitored hourly, and greeted Mr. Daytona in the next bed with a broad 'good morning.'

Marilyn stayed behind the curtain with the Strange Fellow. His arm had slipped from his side and she tucked it up into the sheets and nestled his head properly in the pillow. He roused from the painkillers enough for her to see his blue eyes, young blue eyes and a shock of blonde hair above the limp frame that was like Dad's when Marilyn helped him onto the commode.

On the bedside table there was a card trimmed in pink tinsel and a single, fading rose in a Vegemite jar.

The blue eyes were lost to recognition, but Marilyn looked into them nevertheless. She pushed the hair to the side and patted the jaw near the lesion, but not close enough to make more pain.

When the letter came from the Area Health Service Marilyn called a staff meeting. It was a bright day, so at the last minute she rescheduled to the staff courtyard, leaving only two nurses on the wards for thirty minutes.

When they had gathered, the great gossipy crowd of them, Marilyn walked from the garden into their midst. In the sudden silence she spoke.

'We will treat these men like they are suffering any communicable disease. Remember your malaria training, those of you who have been malaria trained, and use universal precautions for that. If anyone has any concerns with my directive, then I will accept your resignation before the start of your next shift, effective immediately.'

She addressed maintenance on their afternoon tea break, with a simple request that was to be completed before the end of the week: the conversion of the now unused third operating theatre into a special ward for patients selected by Matron. Any queries would need to be directed to her, otherwise work was to commence that day.

The next month, a Strange Fellow died in that room with his family at his side. His sister came to see Marilyn afterwards. They were staying at the motel on the road out of town, and she wanted to thank Marilyn before they left.

'We heard you weren't turning people away ...'

'No dear,' Marilyn said, 'we don't ever turn people away.'

When Mona from the supermarket had this from Beryl at the hospital canteen, neither lady declared they would be telling Marilyn's mother if they saw her at the Bowling Club fundraiser.

THE interstate Night Supervisor resigned that year, and to her surprise Marilyn saw Pam's application on her desk and signalled to the Recruitment Office that if there were no other internal applications then the position would be offered without external advertising.

She'd seen little of Pam, but knew this new job meant the daughter was also destined for the expensive private school. Pam had been a permanent on night duty for three years now, the pros and cons of which they discussed the few times they crossed paths. Marilyn always took the lead in these conversations, letting the other woman know that night duty was not a career dead end or a soft option. Marilyn certainly avoided ever being touched again.

She found the funds for a new office for Pam a few doors down from her own, with similar black letters for her name on the door. Annoyingly, the company who made the letters didn't make exactly the same ones anymore.

Dad got lost the next year. When Marilyn came home Mum was frantic on the verandah and they both got in the car even though Mum was in her dressing gown. They found him down by the river trying to open his bowels under the bridge, crying because he couldn't. For the first five minutes he didn't know them, and Marilyn saw the look on Mum's face in the rear vision mirror, a mixture of love and horror, with Dad's sobbing head in her arms.

She taught Mum how to change his incontinence pads and give him the fig paste to keep him regular. The pads came from the supply in the nursing home, and Marilyn justified it by reminding herself that she'd been her parents' sole carer for many years now, and she knew how much money that was saving the Area Health Service. Plenty more than the cost of a bag of incontinence pads every week or two.

Strangely it was Mum who went first, in her sleep. Marilyn didn't find out until after work and Dad was rambling about the house looking for a feed with Mum dead in the bed, having passed while doing up one of her shoes.

Marilyn called the undertakers, not the ambulance. She knew what was needed, and not to waste resources. Mum's body was cold, beyond laying out. No chance to make her nice with a clean towel rolled up under her chin. She held Dad away as he questioned why these men were taking a large black bag across the kitchen on a trolley, full of his wife of fifty years.

One of the undertakers told one of the wardsmen at Emergency that 'there was shit all over that house, from the front door to the bedroom.'

Until Dad went, Marilyn didn't grieve for either of them. There seemed no need while Dad kept searching for Mum as though she really was still alive and just on her way home to him. Marilyn believed it too some days. She'd stopped putting him to bed and just locked him in the kitchen with the oven turned off at the circuit, thinking *Mum'll take care of him.*

Luckily, before autumn was over, he suffered a lethal stroke sitting up in a chair at the table.

Marilyn had two days off.

Pam had the news from one of the night girls. To their unspoken shame they'd missed the mother's funeral because no one knew she'd gone until well afterwards. Marilyn hadn't said anything, after all.

There was no mention in the paper, and the funeral parlour said they couldn't give out any personal information. 'The only family member has requested no funeral,' was all they said.

Pam thought about it before going to work that night. It must be tomorrow, because the roster said Matron would be in late.

Heading to the cafeteria for a coffee at four in the morning, Pam let herself into Marilyn's office. The room was brutally empty. In the half light, Pam spotted the one photograph on Marilyn's desk, her Mum and Dad, with Pam's two boys on their knees, all smiling.

Pam collected three of the girls at nine and they headed for the cemetery with takeaway coffees, laughing about staking out a funeral.

The day was one of those squally days bringing in the winter, and the damp red leaves of maple trees flecked across dark gravestones.

After thirty minutes, during which they listed everyone they knew who was buried in there, the hearse finally arrived followed by a noble-looking funeral car. These girls, all now pushing fifty, pulled their shawls and scarves over their heads and walked in a phalanx towards the car. One of the funeral men met them half way, his arms outstretched, trying to explain before he opened his mouth: 'She won't let us take the coffin out until you leave.'

'Can I see her?' Pam asked, exhaling a thin anger.

He shook his head. 'It's what she wants.'

They shrugged, and retreated. Marilyn watched them go, her cheeks burning from crying, until the stupid orange car had turned back onto the main road into town.

They put Dad next to Mum and Marilyn stood for an hour after the grader did its work, before the man came to tell her they had to use the car for another funeral.

THE road out of town was widened over a ridiculously long period for the next three years, and the old hospital sign was replaced with a new one that no one could read, all slate and corrugated iron.

The jeweller Brian Ward was killed by a truck on the highway as he was walking back to his car with a jerry can of fuel from the new service station.

Marilyn laid out his tubby little body and after spotting the gold wedding band, rang the wife who was now living in the city. Lynne remembered Marilyn, and said she'd tell the kids, who were all out of university by now, a lawyer and two teachers, 'not the least bit interested' in coming back to the town of their birth, or their father's funeral, Marilyn suspected.

She had the house repainted, during which the workmen found a box of magazines in the wall of Dad's shed when they patched it. They laughed at the mouldy old muscle-man porno, and left them for Marilyn to find months later when she tried to clear some things out for the op shop.

She pushed them back under Dad's work bench, meaning to deal with them on garbage night.

Things were moving on the new ward at the hospital, joined to the Edwardian building with a state-of-the-art covered concrete bridge over the road into the hospital grounds. There were meetings to attend and sometimes she saw Pam, who was also on the board of the nursing home and fundraising for the blood bank.

One morning, on arriving in her office, an envelope greeted her written by hand. The contents yielded no evidence of the writer, but said, simply: 'There is nonsense going on here at night and if nothing is done I am going to report the people involved to the Area Health Service.'

Marilyn got herself a coffee first, then phoned Pam's office to ask her to pop in before leaving, 'today, please.'

She showed Pam the letter the minute she came in.

'It doesn't make any sense,' Pam said, totally innocent. 'What do they think is 'going on'?'

'Perhaps you need to see if your staff are happy?' Marilyn suggested.

'I will,' Pam said, shrugging, 'but I can't think what it could be.'

The next morning there was another note, reading: 'It's disgusting and something should be done about it'. Marilyn called Pam at home, apologising for waking her up, but alerting her to the new situation.

'How are things?' Marilyn asked.

'The kids are all well,' Pam recounted. The boys were both in the city, and the little girl had only a year or two left at school. Pam sounded distant. 'I have done some asking around, but no one's saying anything.'

Marilyn attended work that night at about midnight. Fooled into her route from the old days, she found herself unconsciously seeking out her old office, but the new entrance to the hospital was on the other side.

Just as she decided to go back, the sight of people inside through the plate glass of the new ward mesmerised her. Here and there, moving between rooms, were staff going about their business. Some patients were awake in the light of televisions. Nowhere was there anyone unhappy or a sign of discord, only a hospital quiet and functioning as it should.

Then she spotted Pam, walking across the enclosed concrete bridge, then running, then moving her arms and a ball left her grip. Across the way another nurse hit the ball with something like a bat. Distant laughter, girlie laughter.

They dispersed. Marilyn tutted. Then she saw Pam again, not bowling now but walking at pace, checking on rooms. The hallways ran on and on and Pam travelled quickly along them.

Marilyn knew the look of someone being furtive. Pam turned a corner, disappeared for a moment against the dark lunch room, then appeared again under a light, checking to see if she was being followed. Marilyn assumed she was about to keep walking, but she turned back towards the lunch room and didn't reappear.

Marilyn's mouth was dry and she could smell laughing gas.

She started running without knowing, back towards the entrance, rose thorns dragging across her fat stockinged legs. Then she realised that if she were to get around the other side and into the hospital and back along that corridor to the dark lunch room, Pam would already have shown her breasts and it would be over.

In her bedroom at the end of the verandah, Marilyn rubbed

herself for an hour before she climaxed for the first time in her entire life, hitting her head hard on the headboard as images of Pam swirled in her vision and the wet between her legs spread to her hand.

'If you want to know the truth,' Pam said the next day. 'I've been letting two young staff work on their uni assignments while they're on the ward. It doesn't happen every night, and I keep a careful eye on it.'

Despite her explanation a third note came the next week, followed the next day by Pam's resignation.

Marilyn grappled invisibly when she read the letter. Pam's office was already empty. The Recruitment Office had already processed a request for final pays. Marilyn repeatedly looked up Pam's number until she knew it by heart. She rang once and when the daughter answered, Marilyn hung up.

Pam must have gotten a new car because she never saw the orange station wagon these days.

Marilyn drove down the street where she thought they lived, but there was no sign. She'd gotten the house wrong, or the street, or both. Pam had never invited her over and the Pay Office would not release any details.

MARILYN joined the Quota Club but stopped going after three meetings. She'd never heard such nonsense and the older women looked at her with a kind of indifferent sympathy. The younger women were too young to know who she was, and when one assumed she was new in town, Marilyn pretended to go to the bathroom and never went back.

The Recruitment Officer had his leaving party, annoyingly, during the afternoon, and it spilled out into the hallway outside Marilyn's door. There were balloons and streamers and someone brought her in some cake. Towards the end of her shift, he popped his head in.

'Must be something in the cordial,' he slurred, 'but I just wanted to tell you, Matron ... Marilyn. I wanted to tell you how much we all appreciated that you didn't, you know, turn anyone away when the crisis was taking off.'

Marilyn protested with her body, but he persisted: 'You were one in a million Marilyn. We owe you a lot, and we'll never forget you.'

He was almost cross-eyed, but she could finally see what had always bothered her: the shiny hair, the pursed lips, the swagger.

She simply smiled and nodded, until his drunkenness drew him back into the corridor where the music was blaring and people were laughing.

When she left she had to pass through the bedraggled remnants of the party. He saw her leaving and waved with a knowing nod. She froze her face and disappeared.

She took a week off the next January and went to the city. Dad had always talked about the Australian Museum and the fossils.

She paid the money for the bus trip and booked a hotel, right on Hyde Park, and, after catching a taxi to the Museum, was piqued to see it was only across the park, and blamed the taxi driver.

She couldn't find the fossils but saw the skeleton of a man sitting in a chair with one of a dog sitting next to him, and thought of Dad and Maggie, but couldn't let the feelings out and had a hot chocolate in the cafeteria.

Some kiddies pointed at her and she lipread them saying: 'Look at that fat lady.'

SOMETIME that year one of the older nurses was talking about Pam. She'd had surgery in the city. They'd found cancer. Chemotherapy. Marilyn asked Devine what he knew, even though it's 'not usual to request such information'. He did not smile, said she had two months, was going to die at home.

Marilyn couldn't ring.

The morning of Pam's funeral she sent a bouquet of flowers. White freesias and lavender, specially requested. The exquisite bouquet sat only metres from Pam's coffin.

Retirement meant a party, and Marilyn could think of no way to avoid it. She endured with cups of cordial, and people endured by only coming for twenty minutes then excusing themselves back to the wards, since if anyone would understand that, it was Matron.

There was a letter from the board and the Area Health Service, which spelled her name incorrectly, which was repeated on her last cheque so she couldn't bank it for weeks until it was sorted out.

THE next year, Marilyn went back to the hospital for the annual fête, and, as she passed from the white elephant stall towards the chocolate wheel, two young people spoke her name.

'We're Pam's kids,' the boy and girl said, probably the middle boy. Both tall, like That Man.

'Oh yes?' she said, freezing over.

'How are you, Aunty Marilyn?' the girl said, a vision of her mother.

'Well,' Marilyn said, turning away.

The chocolate wheel was not in its usual place by the rose garden. She'd say that was why she excused herself and moved away so quickly, if anyone asked.

TWO years later, Marilyn found herself in a ward of the new hospital on the fringe of the city.

She'd felt wobbly digging weeds out of the front lawn and a neighbour drove her into emergency after finding her slumped against the fence.

'Don't be ridiculous,' she said in the blur of nurses' hands and arms over her on the gurney as she was thrust into the ambulance.

She waited for her surgery for over forty-eight hours, during which she managed to clean the four-bed room with paper towel from the nurses' station in the hallway, pulling her intravenous drip along on its trolley behind her.

She straightened the charts at the foot of each bed, and checked the vital signs of an older woman opposite.

Two hours later, as Marilyn predicted from the weak and intermittent pulse, Mrs Crabbe died. Her body was discovered when the morning nurse came on duty.

As Marilyn was wheeled into theatre, an Asian nurse with a clipboard asked her: 'Please tell me what procedure you having done today?'

Marilyn was so shocked by the question she could only indicate her stomach with a vague wave of her hand.

The nurse nodded to the orderlies and signed the form for her.

As she lost consciousness, Marilyn noticed there was dust on the chains of the fluorescent lights above the operating table.

HER hands felt for the drainage bag at her side. Nearly full. Very little feeling in her toes.

Bowel cancer, she guessed.

For a day afterwards, she felt the pain, sending out its threads into her body from her belly.

The face of the familiar Asian nurse came and went and then came no more. Marilyn was sure she heard the other nurses referring to her as Butterfly, but that couldn't be right.

She must have been asleep when the doctor came to see her on his rounds the first time.

The next morning she heard him pass the end of her bed and speak to another patient. When Marilyn tried to speak, Butterfly descended and started sponging her face.

That afternoon, they wheeled her into a private room at the end of the corridor, the sharp light startling her so that she had to shut her eyes.

She slept a little before dinner, wondering if she was still nil-by-mouth. Her arms had become so numb she couldn't feel for the drip on the back of her hand. She would ask someone about that.

Surely she shouldn't be so sleepy?

The anaesthetic must have been too strong. She'd ask the doctor if perhaps she'd been given too much, and shut her eyes against the feelings rumbling up from inside.

In her will, Marilyn left instructions for her burial in the plot with her parents. The arrangement had been made so long beforehand that it predated a new council regulation about plot numbers, and space could not be found anywhere near them.

Knowing there would be money in the estate (the house was already on the market), the funeral director asked for special permission to bury Marilyn on top of both her parents.

Mrs. Bethany, who still lived by herself behind Marilyn's house, had it from Colleen Bradman at cards, whose son worked for the excavation company with the cemetery contract, that for a brief moment, as they lowered Marilyn's coffin, it seemed about to break through the smaller ones below.

'Make it quick,' the funeral director had apparently said, as he locked eyes with the digger operator.

HILDA STARTED DRINKING the same year she knew she wanted to dance, right after Aunty Dolly took her to the Shirley Temple flick with the little dog like Boney, Hilda's very own fox terrier.

Boney was a bit deaf but he was still quick on his feet. If Hilda spoke with a squeal in her voice he would wag his tail and put his front legs on her knees and dance with her. He was only in the dance at the start, and then Hilda took it away all by herself, twirling with her arms out and her dress riding high.

But when she asked about dancing lessons, Hil hadn't bargained on Daddy insisting she get up on the table to perform for him there and then right after dinner.

Aunty Dolly looked worried but cleared the crockery. Daddy turned the wireless on, twisting the dials until he found the first music station, and when a slow, strange piece of music began, the likes of which Hilda had never heard, Daddy boomed again: 'Dance, girl!'

Of course, Boney disappeared when she needed him. He knew from experience that clearing the table meant someone was going to look in his ears for mites or clip his nails, so he escaped between Aunty Dolly's legs, out the back door and under the house as she threw the tablecloth into the laundry by the back door and retreated to her little room off the kitchen.

Hilda was about to escape too when Daddy lifted her by her armpits onto the centre of the table, slapped one hand on the dark mahogany and commanded again.

But the music was too slow. Her opening move, patting her knees, must have looked odd without Boney there, but Hilda did it anyway, turning away from Daddy and starting her twirling.

'Is that all?' he laughed, 'is that the best you can do girl?'

Hilda didn't answer. The music was even more sombre now than the droll opening, and the distant voice of a singer was starting to moan.

'Doll, there is no way I am gonna pay for Hil to go to dance classes. She'll never make a go of it,' Daddy said, as he wrenched the wireless knob around to catch the news.

He looked older from this angle, his balding head more obvious, but with his face buried in the paper, ears straining for the latest from the wireless, Hilda could still imagine he was the King.

She slid off the table, and before going to say night-night to Dolly, Hilda spied Daddy's drink on the sideboard, a chunky beaker of liquor. She gulped, stifling a cough as the acid hit her soft palate.

Another gulp, and the dance, Daddy's booming voice, Aunty Dolly, and night-nights were all forgotten.

THE next time Hilda danced was in the bar at Mount Victoria railway station during the second war.

A young officer hadn't even asked her if she wanted to, he just grabbed her off her stool where she was watching the crowd with a group of her friends from the barracks, all having a drink on their way home from Lithgow to Sydney on leave.

He glided her around and she seemed to land in all the places he wanted her to. He even touched her face with the side of his when the music slowed down, and winked at her when he dropped her onto the train as it was pulling away. He gave her as much physical affection as she'd ever had, over the space of half an hour in a crowded railway café where they played music to those waiting for connecting trains.

That night Aunty Dolly told her she'd meet her husband on one of her trips over the Mountains, 'you just see.'

Dolly was Hilda's late mother's sister, and took it on herself to drill Hilda about men, arming her niece with as much ammunition as she could to ensure that the next generation of women did not miss out on good blokes because of a war, just like she had.

Hilda's mum Grace died when Hilda was four, and Aunty Dolly had stayed on in the back room of the house in Strathfield since the family lost all its money in 'The Crash'.

No one would ever explain what that meant, even when Hilda asked, but as she grew into a young woman, she realised that Dad's long hours at the power station and Doll's on other women's ironing barely sufficed to feed the three of them. Even Boney's passing in 1942 had been a blessing to the pantry.

Eventually, Doll's endless education on men paid off.

All her advice on what to say and when to say it turned Miss Hilda Bait into Mrs James Burley at the Strathfield Registry Office in 1950.

Dolly was a resplendent lilac Matron-of-Honour and saved her spare change for months to buy the girl a pure white bouquet of the most perfect roses. Dad wore his Gallipoli medals and was 'proud as punch'.

The Burleys paid for the reception at the pub down the road, with one drink each for twelve (including cousins). Doll and Dad walked home and they both got blisters.

Even though there'd been no music for dancing, everyone said 'a great time was had by all.'

THE Burleys were in furniture, with a big warehouse and factory in Newtown run by two generations.

Family flats were perched on top and all sides, one of which was done out for Jimmie and Hil.

Jimmie's mum Edna Burley (by then a widow) was through the wall. His brother Ned and wife Norma and their three boys were up top with 'views to Bondi'. Two spinster sisters shared a room in with mum.

When Jimmie and Hil came back from their Katoomba honeymoon, Jimmie told his new wife that mum, Barb and Dessie would be listening for sounds of canoodling on the other side of the corrugated walls.

When no canoodling was apparent, and Dessie piped up: 'Perhaps they do it in the kitchen because they know we're listening?' and Edna shooshed her youngest child, Hil and Jimmie had a quiet laugh.

'Mum'll soon tell you all you need to know about the the family,' Jimmie said.

Hil soon learned the Burleys always said what they thought. They'd been in furniture forever and had gradually moved seaward from Auburn towards the Eastern Suburbs 'where all the money is', as Jimmie's Dad Bart used to say.

Newtown was as close as Edna ever wanted to get to the Eastern Suburbs, and, because Sydney Park Road gave the delivery truck easy access from the inner west to the Pacific Ocean, Edna used to add: 'You may as well pay Newtown rent, instead of lining some snob's pocket in Randwick,' against the notion of any further family migration toward the coast.

The Burley boys had been bundled off to Lithgow at the start of the war 'before someone sends them off overseas', old Bart had warned, one of his last wisdoms before a heart attack took him on the factory floor in 1940.

So he never lived to see his youngest lad Jimmie farewelled to the Mediterranean, scrubbing decks in the Navy, or the Jap's raid on Sydney Harbour.

All the business folk of Newtown recalled old Bart's endless assurances that having a factory 'down here away from it all' meant 'your stock was out of bombing range'.

One thing the old man went on about did prove to be true in the end, it had to be said.

Jimmie's boat was hit by the Jerries off Gibraltar, and he spent four days drifting with a few other Allied men before being repatriated to Singapore, only a month before it fell to the Japs, then back into Sydney with a pass for Lithgow again.

Jimmie had watched Hilda many times before he spoke to her. She knew she was too thin for most men, but Aunt Dolly always assured Hilda of the sharpness of her face and the sparkle in her eyes.

Edna said, being the youngest boy, Jimmy was the one Dad made sure to teach some moves to.

The first time Hil saw those moves, she'd fallen for him.

They'd swapped intimate looks between the huts and the barracks. She was learning truck mechanics and packing munitions with girls from the Mountains. He was testing weapons up the hill with a hundred other ruddy-faced lads who were still fit enough to serve, but not right enough in the mind to send back.

They went steady after the war, lost touch with all those 'lifelong mates' in Lithgow, and friendships pledged on the train journey back, and, when Aunt Dolly thought Hilda was old enough at twenty-one, they got engaged.

For the wedding night at The Carrington Hotel in Katoomba, Edna, Dessie and Barb had saved for a room with an ensuite.

Edna told Hil she hadn't wanted 'any girl I knew to have to get ready for her wedding night in a shared bathroom'.

So, Jimmie was able to appear behind Hil when she was getting ready.

She turned and they kissed. He got all excited and she lost her virginity propped up on the sink.

'Now that's done,' he whispered hoarsely, resting his jowls on her face, spotting the blood on his tadger, 'we can do it all night, and in the morning, my girl.'

She liked it better the next morning, and by the time Mum, Barb and Dessie were listening out for the sounds of heads hitting the bed head, Jimmie and Hil had started re-enacting their first time over the kitchen sink, exactly as Dessie imagined, their bits inches above the washing up.

Even though she was soon expecting, Hil was put to work in the accounts office, right through until the week of her confinement. Barb and Dessie worked alongside her, although Barb told her sister-in-law she'd stopped checking Hil's calculations after a week.

Little Eddie wasn't the first Burley grandson so there wasn't much fanfare, but he was the first boy Bait in many a year, so Daddy bought his girl a bottle of French champagne gussied up with a splash of red ribbon, and gave Doll a tiny china dog he'd spotted in the jeweller's window.

He told Hil he'd left it for Dolly on her dresser, right by the mirror, because it was her, not his dead wife and her crazy parents (from out Dural way) who'd given him a legacy.

Hil conceived again the next year, after Jimmie had returned from a sales trip to Canberra.

Another boy – Mark. Jimmie's brother Ned joked his little brother was 'trying to trump three of a kind with one pair,' and he'd better do some swift work in catching up. There was always talk of a Burley branch opening in Melbourne when all the boys grew up.

When Mark was nearly five, Edna decided her daughters-in-law needed a break. She could read that sleepy, almost drunken look of a fatigued young mother like she could read a recipe book, and she had visions of her boys enjoying their wives the way she and Bart had enjoyed one another, so she took the opportunity of sharing her nest egg, which she told everyone she kept shoved in a tin behind the upstairs toilet pipes.

Norma and Ned were treated first, and sent to Kiama at Easter, with the three boys bundled onto the train a week after their parents drove down. Edna had filled them up with food and love, all the while imagining Ned rekindling his love life with the disappointing Norma.

Jimmie, Hil and the boys were treated to Ned's car at the start of summer, down to the Murray River for a fishing holiday.

'There's not a person to be seen all day,' Edna announced, thoughts of her boy getting a leg over at the same secluded spots she had given herself to Bart after he'd come home from Turkey, his neck ruddy from scabies, but his bits clean and primed like a well-oiled engine, long before they were called into any procreative action.

Edna announced they'd regret ignoring her advice and taking the kids with them.

After Canberra (where Ned had made Jimmie promise to 'look in' on furniture suppliers) the roads were not so new. They lunched at the Dog on the Tuckerbox at Gundagai, and Jimmie held both his boys up to see the bronze puppy. About five miles from the Murray they bought a little dog off the side of the road, the naughty kelpie Eddie pointed to, and said they'd pick him up on their way back through the next week.

They reached the mighty river by four. It was January, so it was light for ages. Jimmie said they'd find a camping spot later.

'Let's have a bite eh?' and they picnicked, the heat of the day sending drifts of warm, damp air across the water over all four of them, the sound of crickets already driving all thoughts from their heads.

Jimmie woke first.

A crow had called when it rose off a ploughed paddock on the far bank. He could hear the water sliding past. Mark was snoozing by his head, between his Mum and Dad, and Jimmie felt the wonderful permanence of that.

Hil put her head up, her hair falling out of her 'smart do' and onto the side of her face, pressed with a pattern of grass where her cheek had touched the ground and not the picnic rug. She laughed when her husband blew a kiss for her, smoothed Mark's hair and turned to find Eddie.

Not on the rug, so surely on the slope?

Not there either, or the car.

Jimmie called for him, but only the sluicing of great currents of water answered him.

Hil checked the back seat for the hiding boy, ready to smack for bringing these feelings into her guts, while Jimmie jogged up and down both ways.

There was another car by a shelter up the road, but they'd not seen a little boy.

By seven the police from Wangaratta arrived and Hilda heard someone say: 'Dragnets, up by the reeds,' and she put her head into her lap in the front seat of the car, until Mark started to cry at the approaching night.

Barb took the call from the Gundagai police station and relayed it around the warehouse. Edna made Dessie pack up the little boy's bed and clothing. They would be arriving back, only three of them, by lunchtime the next day.

Barb thought to call Dolly and Hil's father that night, hoping they'd already been told, but they hadn't, so she bit her lip at the silence down the phone line. They'd had to go to a neighbour's place to get the call. 'So someone's with you?' Barb confirmed, and hung up.

Ned's peppermint green Holden slid into the factory drive about three o'clock. Lunch was spoiled and long gone. Edna folded Hil into her arms, like holding a railway sleeper covered in a sheet, and handed her on to Dessie.

Then the older woman took little Mark from the arms of her son, whose face was raw with the shock, like it had been slapped repeatedly.

Little Mark announced: 'We're getting a puppy,' but neither Hil or Jimmie could explain.

There was no body, so there was no funeral. A note came from the Wangaratta police with instructions on how to create a death certificate, and how long to wait before applying, but it was filed in the kitchen with the recipes and the newspaper clippings and forever after forgotten about.

Edna waited a full month before taking Hil by the shoulders and shaking the words: 'Time for another little one now Hil,' into her. Years later, she admitted she'd said: 'Give her another one' to her son after only a fortnight.

Although it took until the following summer, Jimmie did, as they lay holding one another, her back to him, on the bed, while everyone was either at church or out visiting.

A little boy came with the new decade. There was a big christening in Newtown and Hil paid for a new dress for Aunty Dolly. They named him Bartholomew Ian, and everyone squeezed in for a photograph on the church steps.

Hil looked angular. The breastfeeding was making short work of her last maternity fat. In the snap of the moment, she welded her hands to this new little one.

JIMMIE announced to his family that they were moving to Bondi. He'd already put down the deposit on a brown brick semi two streets back from the beach on the hillside, where properties were cheaper, but you got more of a sea breeze. Edna didn't speak to him for a month.

Dessie and Barb would not be moving into the spare flat – that was already rented out, and the money was going to send Ned's and Jimmie's boys to private boarding school. Edna could already smell the scents of the Sixties, and she feared what it would bring to her brood of growing grandsons.

Hil could breathe at last.

She sunned her bones in the concrete courtyard of their new home as the furniture was brought in.

Mark ran about, still pretending to have the dog he'd long heard about, and baby Bart seemed even fresher and newer away from the damp lanes of Newtown.

Jimmie hadn't yet told any of his family about the extra loan for the new showroom in Waverley, and the new contacts in Melbourne.

'Ned's got his secrets, don't you worry,' he repeated to his wife, still worried about betraying his brother and his mother. It was Dad, a second son himself, who gave him the idea and most of the money, years ago.

The Bondi Burleys got browner and healthier than the Newtown mob. Edna passed in 1964, infamously choking on a boiled sweet when she was shouting at Dessie to come inside and do the beans for tea.

She left money to all her grandkids as legacies none of her children could get their hands on.

She'd predicted in 1959 that Norma would end up leaving Ned, an event which came to pass by 1970, but Edna didn't foresee the collapse of the dining setting market, which Ned averted by doing kitchen makeovers and Jimmie was immune to in Lounge Suites and Home Bars.

Dolly got to see her niece more now that she no longer had to steel herself against the Burley family for a visit. Once, sitting in the sun on the terrace, Hil was afraid her aunt would confess that she and Daddy had been sleeping together for years. Everyone from their part of Strathfield already knew.

At Daddy's funeral in 1971, Mark and little Bartholomew were dressed so finely that Dolly cried.

Mark was almost through private school courtesy of his grandmother, and Hilda made him hold his little brother's hand all day, while she was left to continually reassure Dolly that she'd have enough money to get a flat in Bronte with the sale of the Strathfield house.

Bartholomew started dancing for his Great Aunt once she arrived in the Eastern Suburbs.

Doll knew talent when she saw it. She also had a record player, with which she encouraged the boy into wilder and more expressive moves underneath the large archway between her living and dining rooms.

It gave her no end of entertainment, and a new role in her life on the ridges facing the ocean, away from the landlocked inner west.

Even when there was a temporary cessation in classes after Bartholomew fell off Doll's balcony recreating the chimney sweeps' dance from *Mary Poppins* and broke his arm, Dolly took delight in reminding her niece of her own dancing ambitions of years ago.

But nothing could break Hilda's sense of panic about her son's accident.

So, for once, Doll forgot about encouraging Hil to rein in some of the boy's more awkward and 'flamboyant' demeanour when he wasn't dancing. After all, Hil often reminded everyone she'd lost enough over the years.

Jimmie wasn't going so well selling the Eastern Suburbanites expensive furniture they either didn't want or could get cheaper from department stores.

He tried stocking exclusively for Parker Furniture, but he was unwilling to tout for trade in the growing Western Suburbs, which a Melbourne franchise manager had encouraged him was 'a golden market'.

The one time he tried, Jimmie got lost in the truck out at Badgery's Creek. Unless he was driving along routes his Dad had carved out in the inner west or the Eastern Suburbs, he was all at sea.

'The worst thing that could happen to furniture,' Ned said, 'is the department store which also delivers,' and indeed, nothing seemed to go Jimmie's way after the initial flush of the Bondi move.

AUNT Dolly died of breast cancer in 1974. Her flat, which Hil had purchased for 'next to nothing' a few years before, was now worth 'a small fortune', and meant Hil and Jimmie could move again, this time into a much larger house in Double Bay, long before it got exclusive.

Little Bart had a large bedroom on the first floor, and Dolly's record player. With his brother rarely at home, he had the space to choreograph to his heart's content.

But Jimmie was home more than he used to be, and the music bothered him, so Hilda decided to send Bart to Miss Vivienne's ballet classes, a ten-minute walk away.

He took to it so well that long before the end of the year, Miss Vivienne spoke to Hilda of sending the boy to Melbourne to attend the Australian Ballet School.

But Jimmie got angry at the very thought.

'That poofter Parker rep was from Melbourne,' and, 'I'll put him in the army before I send him to a bloody poofter school,' was his response, making the house quiet until Hil emerged from the kitchen and threatened to talk to a lawyer about accessing Edna's money.

'She wanted the boys educated better than you and Ned were,' she said, and there was another big row. Bartholomew hid under the verandah.

Hil told Jimmie he was 'a failure as far as furniture was concerned,' and wanted to add that she'd been to a women's group where they'd said that a pattern of sex over a kitchen sink was a symbol of female suppression, but left it at 'the kid should dance if he wants to, he's good enough!' before the door was slammed and the house went quiet, this time for good.

BARTHOLOMEW went to Melbourne aged just seventeen. He may as well have gone into the army, because when he came back for the Christmas holidays at the end of first year, he looked as strong as a new recruit, an illusion broken every time he moved and opened his mouth.

One night, while he was performing in the ballet chorus at the Opera House, Hil made a pretence of cleaning his room and found the letters shoved under Bart's pillow. She'd seen them arrive, one every couple of days, signed on the back in a beautiful hand, by a 'Mr. Frizelli'.

'It'll kill your father,' Hilda said when Bart returned and attacked leftovers from the fridge.

'He's just one of the teachers,' Bart said, mouth full. 'He used to be a soloist, in Europe,' he added, as though that might make a difference.

All Hilda could see was the pedantic line of little crosses – kisses – at the end of every letter.

So she decided from then on to write to her son every week he was away from them, to remind him of his parents and what they expected of him, even when Bart left for a tour to America and Europe.

She wrote to him when each of the dogs died, when Aunty Barb went mad and got carted off to the loony bin, and when his cousins took up the furniture trade with Uncle Ned, but she never heard anything back.

On the odd occasion he was home, Bart bluffed his way through family gatherings, and kept going to the bathroom, even in the middle of a conversation.

After Bart didn't come back to the table one Sunday lunch, Mark said it was drugs, before Hil slapped her eldest harshly across the neck.

Jimmie muttered about selling up and heading north, but Hil

threatened she was staying if he ever did. 'Anyway,' she crowed, 'you're not ever selling this house.'

When the offer came to join a new touring dance company, Bart let the company inform his family they wouldn't see him for two years.

THE week the company returned to perform in Sydney, Bart called Hilda to tell them which night they all had tickets, and they were to bring Auntie Dessie. She was living in Kogarah in a tiny flat and took every chance to get out and about and 'stay interested in things'.

Bart said he'd see them in the foyer afterwards, and stressed that none of them were to come anywhere near the stage door.

The ballet was *Giselle* and Jimmie was gobsmacked, seeing his youngest boy fly through the air above the stage. Dessie star spotted in the crowd at the bar afterwards.

Hil stayed silent, annoyed at her husband and his ridiculous sister wearing a twenty-year-old frock.

They saw Bart for only a minute before the good looking young performers swept him away into the night. Dessie dribbled all over him and tickled him in the ribs like Edna used to, caught for a moment in the current of creativity, buffeted by nubile dancers who slipped through her grasp.

MARK didn't do well enough in his exams to be a lawyer, so he followed Dad up to Coolangatta, married a girl from Brisbane, and they all set up a furniture factory together, even though Jimmie was officially retired.

After they sold the Double Bay house, Hil had a flat in Randwick for almost a year, but after deciding that she was going to end up having to take care of Aunty Dessie if she didn't get away, she headed to Coolangatta too and bought a place around the corner from her husband.

Having Bartholomew stay would complete the picture, and her spirits were raised when she got a call saying: 'We are coming.'

'We' was Bart and his young friend George. Both tanned, wearing white tops which showed their muscles, they arrived and planted themselves on the front terrace, made cocktails, danced to the stereo and encouraged her to join their sinuous movements. After a step or two she always retreated into the kitchen to get another bottle.

In the morning, George had not even slept in the spare room. At first, Hil thought he must've gotten up early and gone for a swim.

But Bartholomew's door was shut until after lunchtime. She heard noises, thinking perhaps she could wake her son with a cup of tea, but the passionate gasps she heard sent her out the door and down to the shops.

In the afternoon, they were on the terrace again, already making a new round of cocktails.

'Hi Hil,' her son chimed at her, skin glowing from being well loved, 'want a daiquiri?'

It was the third time her son had called her by her first name. She'd say something to him about it when he was sober, but he never was.

Mark and Sheila made excuses about not being able to make it across town for dinner, and didn't put in appearance for the whole week.

It rained all weekend, and before the weather could improve, as Hil kept promising it would, the boys slid into their lime green jeep and headed back south.

Six months later, she got a call from Bartholomew.

'He's having an affair,' he blurted.

'Who?' she asked.

'George, of course,' Bartholomew whined, 'he's moving out tonight, and I don't think I can stand it Hil.'

Like Edna before her, Hil knew what to do.

She had plenty of money left from her half of the Double Bay house. What Bart needed was good food and deep healing. Jimmie had never bothered with the boy, that was obviously what went wrong, but Bart was still young enough for her to turn things around.

She'd been to some classes at the Arts Centre, where she met some young local women. There was also the new Healing Retreat, replete with lovely fresh-faced Coolangatta beauties.

Under Hilda's high-set house was a studio where Etherea from the Healing Retreat was recruited to teach healing massage and psychic workshops.

The first night, before Bart even opened his mouth, he descended the stairs and every woman in the place, whether in tie-dyed skirts, with henna hair, wearing shells or just there because she'd been roped in, all of them sent their energy out onto this naturally sinuous young man.

They hovered around Bart, waiting to massage his shoulders or push his legs into stretches as he lay like an offering for them.

His body was beginning to heal from his dark days, and in the meditations he vocalised powerful psychic messages that grew more detailed every week.

All of them paid in advance and came back the next week.

Etherea was pleased. Sales of books and oils in the shop were up, and Hilda didn't charge to use the room underneath her house.

By the end of his first year away from the city, Bart decided to change his name.

After years of jokes about 'Bartholomew Burley', he decided to 'attract some positive energy into my consciousness.'

He did his numerology, consulted his cards, and asked his psychic guides about the final decision, before settling on Bart Boston.

It had a ring, and a ring wasn't bad for someone who planned to turn his back on ballet and try his luck in show business.

Not long after that, Hil decided she would attract some positive energy into her consciousness and change her name too.

The irony of Hilda Bait becoming Hil Burley was something she'd never been able to shake off. In her women's group a decade before she had entertained passing as Hilda Burley-Bait. Now, with Etherea's help, she announced from henceforth she'd be known as Joy Day.

BART didn't talk much to Joy about going around to Dad's. Jimmie was getting doddery, and his youngest son explained he was helping his father keep the place clean.

Hil tried to warn him that all they'd have in common was chit-chat about the amazing views and the weather, and that soon enough Jimmie would bore Bart by regaling him about the Burleys and their fortunes.

Jimmie always lied about his 'tall, strong Dad, a man who could lift a wardrobe by himself' when Hil knew clear as day that old Bart was short and wiry and not in the least heroic. Edna had told her all there was to know.

When the visits got more regular, Hil tried to make fun of her husband by saying the stories meant the old man was undoubtedly losing his marbles.

But Bart was pensive. He said his father was struggling and needed solutions to simple things around the house.

Eventually, Bart got an offer of dance work on the Gold Coast. Joy was pleased when he started jogging to get himself into shape instead of spending all that time listening to his Father's nonsense.

Joy had cancelled the healing classes as soon as Bart took up jogging, but she still had Etherea over for psychic readings, and she tried to interest Bart in the news that Etherea reckoned they could contact little Eddie.

'Who's Eddie?' Bart asked, looking for clean towels after a run.

'Your older brother, you know, the one that went in the river?'

When Bart pressed her for more information, coming over all grumpy, she waved him off because she needed to stay calm for her reading.

'Ask your father, since you're getting on so well.'

Later that night, after Bart took hours to return, Hil was waiting for him with half a bottle of wine left and a ruined lasagne.

Dad had told Bart his other brother would have been forty that year.

Apparently, Jimmie had known for years that Eddie hadn't stood a chance against the mighty arms of the river. Four days lost at sea clinging to a bombed-out lifeboat had taught him that. Deep water had a way of grabbing at you. Nothing to be done about it.

'Your Father actually said all that?' Hil asked.

Her son nodded, and, after letting out a snort, she took herself to bed.

When Bart decided to move in with Dad, as usual, he had very little to take with him. He owned only clothes.

According to Mark, Dad had told Bart if he ever wanted to bring 'a pal' home, he didn't have to worry, Jimmie couldn't hear a damned thing through the walls, and Joy laughed and laughed, imagining what Dad would say if Bart ever tried.

As it turned out, Joy waited six months for an invitation to cook dinner for the new fellow Bart had met at the start of rehearsals and was always talking about. She imagined someone like George, only more tanned, more muscled and more distracted.

Instead, the long-limbed Brian kissed her and immediately complimented her on the art on her walls. When Bart mentioned they were her creations, Joy got the most genuinely proffered compliments she'd ever had from anyone.

Barely a month later, Jimmie proudly gave Bart and Brian the twelve-piece Parker dining setting that was 'just sitting in the garage' when Bart announced he was moving into Brian's place.

Joy waited for almost a year for an invitation to come to Surfer's Paradise for the weekend. She wanted to see the boys' 'retro fantasy' for herself, and they had a new puppy.

Her son collected her off the bus, and Brian had lunch waiting, but after showing Joy the place, which was just nothing more than an old beach house, they all returned to the back deck to find the dog finishing off the guacamole.

The boys laughed, but Joy pointed out that if it was her dog, she'd get a smack for that.

They needed to start training the dog then and there, but Brian ruined lunch, dinner, and breakfast out the next morning when he insisted on ignoring her ideas about a training regime for 'Tilda'.

Finally, Brian took the dog on a three-hour walk. When he returned she and her son were sitting on the back deck drinking red wine.

'How's training going?' Joy asked him, but Brian was surly all afternoon and by dinner was almost incapable of talking.

That night, Joy listened to the boys argue in the back room after she went to bed. 'No one ever treats her like that,' her son said.

A YEAR later, the week after Bart was offered the lead in a new show, a stroke took Jimmie in his sleep.

Three men from the bowling club, one of whom survived the sinking off Gibraltar with Jimmie, found their way to the funeral at the memorial gardens. They all shook the boys' hands, but none of them looked Joy in the eye, even when she told them her old name.

Dad left his money to her, Mark and Bart, but she'd announced well over a year ago that she was going to use all of it to renovate Dad's house and build it higher to get the views. She'd paid for architect's plans, after all.

'I've never had much in my life,' Joy reminded the boys, while Brian was clearing the dishes.

So Joy moved across to Jimmie's place and sold hers.

But before the settlement became final, before they got probate for Jimmie's estate, before Bart's show could open, the show which some said was going to be the making of Bart Boston, in the middle of a late-afternoon rehearsal, after complaining of a racing heart, Bart collapsed.

Mark brought Joy to Brisbane to see her son's body. Afterwards. In a motel bath, she went cold, despite the hottest water she could get out of the taps.

They next day, they went to Brian's house. The coffin was in the front room by a wide day bed.

Joy averted her eyes from it, and sat at the Parker dining table.

The funeral director arrived and looked at them all in turn, but she thought he could have looked at her more. She was Bart's mother, after all.

She watched through the door into the bedroom, as Brian picked clothes to bury Bart in.

The funeral director left the house with the clothes over his shoulder. Brian wouldn't settle. He walked from the kitchen to the bedroom.

Finally, he took Mark aside and she heard him say: 'We're having drinks for Bart here, tonight. You are welcome to stay, but if you could get your mother to stop drinking until a bit later ...'

'I'll take her back to the motel,' Mark said, but by the time her son came to find her, Joy was in the car.

The funeral brought Burley cousins from Sydney and even some distant ones from the Bait side who'd heard for years about their famous dancing cousin. Joy told Dessie not to bother making the trip.

Brian spoke. They clapped him. He spoke of a man Joy didn't know. What Mark said about his brother was much better.

They burnt Bart's body. He'd been stiff and cold when she saw him, after the autopsy. Wasn't him. Etherea said sometimes people could wake up after dying. There'd been a case in Canada recently.

The next day, Joy waited in the car while Mark ran across the road in the rain to collect the dog. No one answered the front door.

'Go around the side and call it,' Joy said, getting terse at the way her son's hair was slicked over his nose.

Mark paddled back across the road. He emerged from the thick palms by the house, and shrugged.

'Must be out,' was all he said, getting back into the car. 'We'll drop into the funeral home, and then home.'

The funeral director was polite, but Joy knew the type. He held his hands up when he walked.

'Your son's partner is going to pay for the service, and all the extras,' he said, guiding her to a seat behind frosted glass, 'it's all taken care of.'

'I'll pay for all the funeral costs, right now,' she said, refusing to sit. 'Just send me the death certificate.'

The man fixed her with a neutral stare which she wanted to wipe off his face.

'They weren't partners you know, not like you're imagining,' Joy said. 'I know why *you'd* imagine they were, but they weren't.'

She fumbled her thick purse out of her bag and pushed a credit card across the table. Only when the man processed the transaction did she sit and accept a complimentary cup of lukewarm coffee.

WHEN Mark announced that Brian had called asking for Bart's death certificate, all Joy could say was: 'We don't even know why he died yet, why would he want it?'

A few days later, when Brian called her, explaining he needed the certificate to wrap up his partner's affairs, Joy hung up. Mark got angry, rang Brian and said he'd come by and collect Bart's things, while Joy stood by the phone and made sure her son told Brian that she was having the dog.

Etherea rang, said Brian had called her, but she thought it best she didn't intervene. 'It can muck up the psychic messages,' she said.

Joy made sure Sheila knew that if Brian called her, she should just say he must talk through the lawyers.

When her lawyer asked if she definitely wanted to book a barrister and a court date to prove her son had never been in a relationship with Brian, she didn't notice the surly looking woman had called her Hilda.

Her mind had been wandering dangerously close to the Murray River, and, when it did that, she still knew what to do.

Never, ever, tell Daddy or Edna or Aunt Dolly when and where they had drunk that bottle of French champagne Dad had given her when Eddie was born.

Jimmie had put it on ice bought at the service station, sluiced into the esky at Gundagai.

Life with the Burleys was never relaxing. The world was just learning what relaxation was, so who could blame them, before deciding on a spot to camp, for cracking open the bubbly before they noticed the current?

Eddie was excited about his new dog, dancing up and down by

the water's edge, pretending the puppy was jumping with him, while she ripped off the cork and sloshed the bubbling liquid into coloured anodised cups and offered one to her husband.

The acid of it slid across her soft palate and she exhaled. As she leant on one arm, she saw the bright red ribbon from the bottle fall towards the surface of the water, where it danced lightly, choreographed by a breeze that rose from the speed of the current, before it was sucked quickly from her sight.

They're Curing All Sorts of Things Now

MELBA STARTED TO pretend she couldn't see the scared little kelpie dog. She'd sit with a cup of tea by the front window until he'd creep across the threshold of the back door and drop at the side of her television chair.

Her son Murray was always talking about getting her a dog to give her some company, but Melba just couldn't get her dead husband's voice out of her head.

Norman had endless opinions on the subject of dogs, especially how it was 'not on to feed any dog that didn't earn its keep.'

He was talking about sheep and cattle dogs, of course. They'd had generations of those over the years. Enthusiastic, bright little things, as Melba remembered, but never in the home yard, and shot through the head when they got lame or went after the stock.

Murray knew very well what his father was like. *He might have asked me if I wanted to take on a new puppy*, Melba thought, but she decided to wait until her son said something about it, which he didn't, for a long, long time.

Doggie was nearly fully grown when Melba decided to say something to Murray. They were sitting on the back porch, and the neighbour's cat, a yellow and black feral-looking thing, was helping itself to Doggie's bowl.

'Never gives Doggie a chance,' Melba muttered.

'Eh?' asked Murray, his teacup dangling.

There had been another long silence between them. Murray had his car keys dangling in his other hand. It had been the only sound until the cat's bell made Melba look up.

'The cat, it eats all Doggie's dinner. *Shoo!*' Melba said.

Murray looked tersely at her, clearing his throat the way he'd done since he was a child, when he wanted to say something but couldn't find where to start.

'Greedy thing,' she added.

'How long?' Murray managed, shifting from one side of the chair to the other, making a squeaking sound on the plastic cushion. He gave a little laugh, crossed his long hairy legs the other way, and scratched a red patch on the side of his thigh.

'Hmmmm?' Melba toned, as she'd always done, to get the rest of it out of him.

'How long have you been putting those bowls out Mum?'

'Oh ... since Doggie came along. Must have been sometime after Christmas I should think.'

'Oh, okay then,' Murray said.

She was watching the cat, but she could feel her son's eyes on her. For a moment it gave Melba the oddest feeling, the kind she sometimes got on waking, or when trying to get to sleep on a hot summer night and she wanted to rip off her sweaty nightie and walk naked on the verandah, an approaching storm missing their old property out of town and lighting up the earth far away to their north.

It was a feeling of too much space in the world. The distances between everyone were too big. Right now there seemed miles between her and her son, and the cat was further from her again.

The cat noticed Melba trying to work out how far, and flitted away under the hedge where it had made a hole, which seemed like it might be a day's drive from where Melba sat with an arm on the floral vinyl patio tablecloth.

'Mum?' Murray said, and she was back.

'Yes, dear?' Melba asked, looking him in the eye. Cold and blue, just like his father.

'You know there is no dog, don't you?'

'Isn't there?' she sighed, leaning on her hand and changing her gaze to the climbing rose. It needed a good prune now the weather was changing.

Murray stood slowly, placed his teacup on the tray, and took hers away too. She listened to the rhythm of his hands scrubbing them clean at the sink with the tap going, the way she'd told him not to, for the waste of good water. As his slow footsteps returned, keys jiggled, and he kissed her on the head.

'See you at church Mum,' he said, winked (she didn't look to see that, but knew he did it, even though it made her wince), and strode down the side of the house and away.

Doggie came out the back door once the noise of the car had faded, sniffed the air, and slunk into the green shadows of the table where Dad's shoes were still in untidy rows. Melba could hear him settling under there, moving the shoes into just the right spot.

'You stay,' she whispered, then went for the pruning shears.

'HOW do you get your bulbs to grow so well?' Kenneth asked, once their long, bracing hug had finished, 'they're just marvellous Grandma. The garden's fabulous.'

Melba smiled, her face full of morning sun, and she arched a hand over her brow so she could see the rows of shining daffodils beneath the fir trees that Dad had planted the year they moved off the farm. Kenneth took her other hand, and gently led her along the garden beds, pointing at the clumps of gold.

'You just have to lift them, every year,' she said, 'rest them in an old hessian thingy in the shed, then plant them again before autumn is over.'

'I'm going to do it Grandma, we've got a little patch of garden out the back.'

'They draw the energy into themselves while they're resting,' she explained, 'then they have a new life, better than before. Like magic.'

They made tea together, and ate the cold lunch Melba had prepared at about six that morning while she listened to the news. They'd had good rain overnight. Six millimetres to the north, and Melba had five in her own rain gauge down the back past the clothesline.

Kenneth set the table inside. 'Let's have the good cutlery,' he called, 'do you want to?'

'That would be very nice,' she said. He set a good table. She wished she'd made a hot meal now, but the thought of preparing one had been growing at the back of her mind ever since Kenneth had phoned.

Kenneth showed her into the good room and helped her into her place, and made a big show of unfolding her linen napkin. He poured her a glass of red wine, one hand behind his back, and then one for himself.

'Cheers,' he said, bringing their glasses together gently, and laughing. She laughed too. He rustled about in the kitchen for a few minutes, talking to her from there about the drive up from the city. 'I always forget about the roos,' he called, 'we nearly hit a very large one at the bridge, but lucky for us it was going too fast!' then he reappeared with their plates.

There was stuff on it, and there were slices of bread, and a pile of green with some other stuff dripped across it. 'There we are,' he said, settling in next to her, '*Bon appetit!*'

The taste was lovely. She heard music. The record player in the front room was alive. He must hear it too because he was bobbing his head, and smiling at her, although she did notice him give her a serious look when he thought she wasn't looking. People would do that, and then sneak a look at their watch, but Kenneth never did that. They swayed and bobbed their heads, smiled and ate.

Kenneth asked if he could get some preserved fruit from the laundry shelves for dessert. She said yes, but he came in with just ice cream in blue and white china bowls. While he was rummaging around out the back she thought he might spot Doggie. He sometimes spent the night in the laundry, when the weather was colder, but Kenneth didn't mention anything.

'There's ants out the back, all over those empty dog bowls,' he said eventually, 'shall I wash them up Grandma?'

'I suppose,' Melba said, 'don't put them away though.'

'No Grandma,' Kenneth replied. His mood changed a moment, just long enough for Melba to read it.

'Have you seen your father?' she asked.

He shook his head, looking at the bottom of his empty bowl.

'I only came to see you Grandma.'

'All that way, just for me?'

'I'm heading north for a holiday. I can drop in on the way back in a week or two, if you'd like that. Bring you a souvenir tea towel from the Big Pineapple if you like?'

She smiled and patted the table. It disarmed him and she put her hand on his.

'Your father is a good man. Many people in this town look up to him,' she said.

'I know,' Kenneth answered, head not comfortable in any position. 'Shall we have tea on the terrace?' he finally said, 'and a choccie or two? I'll wash up.'

Mrs. Palmer over the back fence had her classical music records on, and they listened to her singing along, smiling when she tried to hit the top notes. 'Callas,' Kenneth said, 'she was a bit of a screecher herself, especially in her later years.'

He put his teacup down strangely, placing it and twisting it around at the same time.

'There's something I want to say Gran—' was all he could get out before Melba put her hand up. Doggie was coming out of the laundry and walking straight past Kenneth towards her.

'This is doggie,' she said with relief, 'I knew he'd come and see us when he was ready.'

Doggie stayed a bit longer than usual, at Melba's feet. Kenneth looked at her gently, his head on one side. 'He's a very nice doggie,' he said, but he was patting the air in front of him.

A POSTCARD came from Kenneth, with a picture of the Big Banana and the words 'Greetings from Coffs Coast' splashed across it.

Doggie was behind her when she turned back from the letterbox. He skipped out of the way, ran to the front steps and barked. Melba turned to see if there was a cat on the road, or a car coming, but the street was silent. Weekday morning silent. Everyone-was-doing-something-else silent.

She tried to read the postcard before going back inside, but every time she went to, Doggie barked again, from somewhere down the side of the house now. She followed him, but by the time she got out the back he'd disappeared.

The things that went on her face were by her bed, so she went in to get them, because she'd need them to look at the card. She found them, opened them, and put them on, but Doggie barked so loud she thought Mrs. Palmer might make the thing in the other room make the noise.

Melba tutted, and went to give the naughty thing a little wallop, but he was still hiding.

She saw the card the next morning. Doggie had slept on the bed. She felt his warmth when she woke up, and heard him stretching in the half light. For a minute, she wondered why there was a banana on her bedside table, and then she remembered.

She sat up, flicked on the light and read the card.

'Hi Grandma. We're having fun. I'll see you next weekend sometime on the way home. Hopefully Dad will have spoken to you by then, and we can have a good talk. Lots of love Kenny xoxoxoxoxox.'

As the kettle boiled she put the card on the fridge. The thing rang at seven. It was Murray. He was coming around on his lunch break.

'YOU'VE got one too,' Murray announced before he said anything else and flicked Kenny's postcard off the fridge, scanned it, then kissed Melba on the head.

She passed him a plate of sandwiches. He smiled and opened them. The orange things on the inside of the bread didn't seem to be right, and she'd hoped they'd be right, because Murray could get tetchy if his lunch wasn't right. He rummaged for a minute and came back with different things inside the bread while she sat on the porch. Doggie was alert by the clothesline.

'We've had ...' he stopped, waiting for her.

'Hmmm?'

'We've had some news from Kenneth,' her son said between mouthfuls, shuffling in his seat. He reached for the glass of ginger beer and slurped. 'He's asked me to come and tell you, but it's nothing anyone around here didn't already suspect, Mum. He's a homosexual. *A gay*, you know. Reckons he's gonna be happier now everyone knows,' and then he filled his mouth again, looking between her and the food.

She sniffed the air and unfolded her arms. Doggy had moved from the clothesline, and as she went to speak, he ran in a beautiful arc and herded a flock of sheep up onto the porch and through the back door. There must have been eight, ten or more head of them, fleece heavy and ready for shearing. Doggie had them in before she could blink. Murray just munched.

'Do you understand what I said Mum?'

'Yes dear,' she said, sure she'd felt the brush of wool across her knees.

'Now, there's something else ... I've been speaking with Jilly, and she's agreed to come down and go with you and me to the doctor, the day after tomorrow, so he can give you a good check up. She's on her way today, so we can't cancel the appointment. We don't want her to get all annoyed. You haven't been since last year.'

Murray took one more munch and went to scrub the plate. 'Is that all good then Mum?' he called from the hallway, his voice almost drowned out by the sound of sheep herded into a yard.

KENNETH sat across from her. His arms and legs were brown from the sun. He looked more like his grandfather than his father, but he was disappointed. When she said Doggie wouldn't like the toy he brought, she was only telling the truth, he wouldn't like it. He was a working dog, and old Dad said: 'They're not to be mollycoddled.'

He put the fluffy cat toy down on the floor anyway.

'Now, your father has told me all about you,' she said, sugaring the tea and stirring. That made him smile.

'Do you understand?' Kenneth said, taking the cup and trying to look her in the eye, but she was after the thing with the other things on it, the sweet ones, to pass to him.

'I do,' she said, 'and we've all got to put our heads together to help you. You're sick, that's all, and I'm sure there's a cure. They're curing all sorts of things now. If you watch the news there's always a cure for everything, now isn't there?'

'I'm not sick Grandma,' Kenneth said, putting his teacup down and exhaling, 'it's not a sickness.'

Melba looked at her grandson again. He hadn't taken any of the sweet things. His head was down, his fringe was longer than old Dad's had ever been, and his blue eyes were looking at her between the dark strands. Slowly the corners of his mouth came up.

'You're not sick?' she asked. He shook his head.

'I'm fine, in fact it's been the best holiday I've ever had.'

'That's a relief,' she said, 'I've been worrying about you, but I can see you're quite well. That's all I need to know.'

Her grandson smiled more, and took one of those things. 'Biscuits!' she blurted, remembering, shocking him into a laugh.

Later, in the garden, they walked down to say hello to Mrs. Palmer.

'Hello Melba,' she said, rose-patterned gloves matching the carnage she'd wrought on her prizewinning Mr. Lincolns. 'Hello,' she added, for Kenneth, not looking at him at all.

'If my little Doggie ever gets into your yard, you just tell him to go home, won't you, Wilma?' Melba said.

Mrs. Palmer made another cut and a withered rose fell. She nodded, and smiled. As they turned to walk back up to the house she watched, shaking her head.

'How was Aunty Jilly?' Kenneth asked her at the bean patch.

'She's got the girls to take care of, why's she coming?'

'She's already been Grandma, to take you to see the doctor. The girls are both at university now, remember?'

'Oh yes, so they are.'

'You've got some pills to take now, do you remember to take them every day?'

'For my hallucinations, yes.'

'Right, and you're to tell Dad if there's any side effects, or any time when you don't feel quite like yourself. I'll remind you when I call. I'm going to call you every week now Grandma, so you don't go off on a round the world trip or something.'

'I've wanted to, I don't mind saying,' Melba said, 'but I couldn't leave Doggie, you know that.'

'That's right, but if you feel like it, you can always leave Doggie with me.'

'Did you hear that Doggie?' she said, the pup coming to her side and matching her pace.

'IF we don't take this unit, we might have to wait a long time for another one,' Jilly said, her bag stowed firmly under her arm, standing by the window. 'There's a bit of a view. I can see the fields at the back of the Bryant's place. Mum, are you listening? Are the Bryants still over at The Mulgas?'

Melba was listening to her daughter, because she couldn't see much of her, only the red top and the blue pants, and the large limbs that manhandled her across the room. 'Hmmmm?' Melba said.

'Are the Bryants still ...' then a tut, '... doesn't matter. The kitchen's just down the hall, so at least you'll get your cup of tea first in the morning. That's nice, isn't it?'

Melba could feel the bumps of her bedspread from home. Her feet didn't touch the floor, and one of her shoes fell off with a thump. Doggie jumped away and sat by the door, ears flat in panic, listening for something down the corridor.

Jilly tutted again and went for the shoe, jerking it back onto her Mother's foot. 'Murray been to see you yet Mum?'

'This morning, I think,' Melba said. She could see Murray at the gate of the old farmhouse, going off to school, chest stuck out to show off his neatly tied tie.

'Well I'm off to get you some things, some nice toiletries, alright?' and she patted her mother's arm.

Doggie just managed to get himself out of the way, but he wouldn't settle. The sheep were coming, and fast. Melba clutched the bedspread, drawing it to her like a fleece. Doggie licked one of her hands. She could feel his panting on her fingertips.

'Get around behind,' she whispered, and off he ran.

THE black thing rattled. It had rattled earlier but Melba was very far down. Sometimes she swam to the top of the bed and she could stay afloat, but old Dad needed her to hold the gate, so she couldn't get the black thing before.

Now she reached out for it and it made its other noise.

'Grandma? Grandma it's Kenny.'

'Yes,' she said, nodding, 'are you coming?'

'Not today Grandma, I'm at home, in the city, but I am coming to see you for your birthday, which is very soon. How are you?'

'Yes,' Melba said, 'oh yes,' and she wanted to say something else, but there was something at the bottom of the bed. When she looked, she could see Jilly, so she said: 'Jilly's here.'

'Oh, I might have a word with her, in a minute. I hope everything's going okay with your pills Grandma. You must say if they make you feel odd. I'll ask Jilly about it for you, okay?'

'She's here, but it's a *silly Jilly*,' Melba said. Her daughter lay in a ditch by the bed, like a child fallen down a well and laid out in the sun to dry, hair stuck to her head, one eye looking up at the sun, as funny as a clown, but silent.

'Grandma, I think that's just an hallucination, I think ...'

'She's not going to get up, not today.'

'Okay ... okay Grandma. It's okay. Listen, how is Doggie?'

'Oh he's well. They wouldn't let him in, but he comes in anyway. I keep little bits of food for him you know, which he likes.'

'That's nice Grandma. Have you had your lunch today?'

'Yes,' she said, and stopped, because Jilly was just realising how far down she was, and she needed her mother to watch, so Melba put the black thing down so she couldn't hear either of its noises anymore, and waited for Jilly. Doggie would come and lick Jilly's face clean if she whistled for him.

THE bright things filled her whole vision and kept her afloat. Too far away to touch, they seemed to drop away on all sides. At least there was no black. Melba didn't like the black.

Hands touched her since the black went. Held the thing of warm that slid down her throat, and lifted her clear of the ditch to a new soft thing that slid them along.

Doggie couldn't see her for a moment, but the sheep were out so he soon caught up. Old Dad must have left the gate open so he'd be angry at everyone but himself as usual.

Jilly lay by the opening of light. *She'll get used to it eventually* Melba thought.

They slid past and then the light and the sound of rain made by hands hit together on all sides and the bright things before her.

More hands, and faces, looming at her, but friendly. Bristly kisses of men, and pressing.

'It's Kenny,' she heard one say.

'Happy Birthday to you. Always said you'd make it to one hundred,' Kenny said.

She floated all the way up to the surface then, and breathed deeply. He did not stand above her, but crouched down, his smile enveloping her. Everyone else stood at the other end of the room.

'Grandma, I'd like you to meet someone.'

'Hmmmmm?' she said, as another man looked into her.

'This is Greg,' Kenneth said.

Another face, both of them held together, smiling. 'Happy birthday Melba.'

Melba looked for Doggie. He sat at Kenneth's feet, waiting for scraps. Everyone else was so very far away, like neglected food on the far side of a plate.

'Whose boy is he?' Melba called.

'Greg is Deirdre's boy, and he's my boy too,' Kenneth said, enfolding her in his arms and staying there. Melba felt like she used to when old Dad shut the door and whispered in her ears things he never said on Sundays.

'Look what we have for you,' came another voice. Jilly, but not the silly one in the ditch. Then paper and more bright, and two other faces. Young. No bristles.

'Say Happy Birthday to Grannie,' Jilly said. *Happy Birthday Grannie!* they all chimed.

In front of her was all nice, and hands helped her with more nice that went inside her, and then wiped, but on the edges it wasn't so nice. Jilly was talking.

'... Needn't have brought him here,' she said, 'to make a fuss when it's not about you Kenny, it's about family being here to celebrate Mum's big day.'

'Nice to see you too Aunty Jilly.'

'Don't you play all polite with me. Go and talk to your father for once.'

'The girls have brought their boyfriends.'

'That's not the point,' Jilly said, wiping Melba's face repeatedly. Melba wanted to say something, but with all the wiping, all she could do was start swaying instead.

ONLY a nurse clearing Melba's tray heard the words when they finally arrived, ten minutes later.

'You're so *special*!' Melba blurted.

'Oh thank you, Mrs. Reed, that's very nice of you to say,' the nurse said, misunderstanding as she cleared Melba's drink and wiped the tray.

Most of the family heard. Kenny pressed his boyfriend's hand.

'Can we go?' Kenny appealed, face red with the heat. 'She's the only one who's ever honest about anything, and they've doped her up to the eyeballs'.

Then Melba started. It was barely audible at first, just a muttering that nobody in the lunchroom of the nursing home would have given a second thought to.

But it quickly grew louder, and when she couldn't find her cup to drown the beat out of her, Melba began to slap her hand on the smooth formica of the tray.

By then, everyone could hear her quite clearly. With her only daughter under her gaze, the old woman was shouting: 'Silly Jilly, silly Jilly, silly Jilly, silly Jilly, *silly Jilly*!', and she started to scream it, the juice that stuck to her throat making it into a guttural chant, as the nurse wheeled her back to her room.

People closed the gap left by the birthday girl's removal, looked at watches and glanced at the clock.

Jilly's mouth formed into the same smile she'd used when her daughters wet their pants in public, or when her husband vomited in the RSL car park after the footy. She knew if she looked at Kenneth, she would lose.

'We'll have to watch that nurse when Mum's time comes,' Jilly whispered to her eldest, 'they say family *hair-looms* go missing in nursing homes. It's usually the nurses. The ones who think the oldies really give a damn about them.'

The daughter nodded. 'Find your sister,' Jilly said, 'I want to be on the road in five minutes.'

AFTER Jilly's funeral a week later, the Country Women's Association put on morning tea. Kenny flew up from the city without Greg.

The girls were haughty and monosyllabic in their grief, both with bandaged foreheads and a young man tagging after them.

Kenny tried to mingle with his father, who hopped from one foot to the other whenever anyone mentioned his sister's name.

He ended up chatting with a cousin from out west, pretending to be fascinated in the journey between this out-of-the-way Queensland town, and the place where this man had carved out an existence as a combine harvester salesman.

He ran into his father coming out of the toilet, and enclosed him in a hug before the other man could escape, but Dad went like a board.

'Does Grandma know?' Kenny asked.

Dad's jaw dropped. 'No, she doesn't, and I don't want her to either, it'll kill her, you know that.'

'Dad, they say with vascular dementia that it's not a case of not understanding things. She's bound to notice if her only daughter doesn't come to visit anymore ...'

His father struggled with the information, mouth open, eyes straining.

'I'll tell her,' Kenny said.

'You ...' Dad said, leaning against the wall for a second, then taking his own weight again.

'Hmmmm?' Kenny encouraged.

'You live too far away,' and he brushed himself down and was gone.

Kenny nodded goodbyes to the girls and called a cab for the dusty airport, where he exchanged his return flight for a hire car and got on the road.

By eight he was across the border in an empty motel.

He got up before the sun and breakfasted at a truck stop. Five kilometres further was the place where Jilly collided with a roo and rolled the van on her way home from Grandma's birthday.

Both the girls and one boyfriend were asleep in the back, which is why the police reckoned they survived.

The tracks of emergency vehicles still showed in the red dirt either side of the road, and the trail where the tow truck had hauled the bent vehicle out of the ditch.

There was a distinct scent in the air: rotten roo flesh. A hum of blowflies led him across the ditch and into the yellow knee-length grass. Surely someone would have removed the roo by now?

No, there it was, a dusty pelt the size of a boulder with its side clobbered in. Paws in supplication and head thrown back like a prostrate dog watching for its dinner. No blood. Jilly must have swerved to avoid it.

Silly Jilly.

Five minutes later, thinking about why he had not one tear in his dusty eyes, Kenny worked out that his Grandmother already knew Jilly was dead, without anyone having to tell her.

THERE were rows and rows of daffodils in the field, making a golden hillside out of their old farm.

Doggie stood by the gate, so Melba knew her journey was going to be safe.

Old Dad's been leaving it open all these years for a reason, she thought.

The road looked like their old driveway, but not exactly, cutting as it did through daffodils that Melba was sure she'd never planted.

There were sheep roaming in the field up above, their fleece showing above the golden glow of the flowers, but there was a storm brewing behind her, and Doggie was bristling to get going.

'Not yet boy,' she whispered, her voice disappearing into the rustling of the flowers.

Up near the top of her blankets, Melba waited for her last pill.

They said Kenny was coming, but they always said someone was coming.

When the pill came, washed down with warm stuff, the cup was a baby's with handles like silly ears either side, only Melba was holding neither.

The pill slid deep inside her, and, as Melba closed her eyes, she felt it whipping up the storm with strikes of lightning that whitened the landscape in bursts.

Doggie spooked, but stood firm.

A sound came from deep within the earth. Something told Melba not to listen with her ears, but to let herself sink from the lip of the blanket into its fibres.

She started to disappear, as the ancient voices rose and filled the storm with nascent power placed right into Melba's hands, which seemed as though they'd be solid for a few more moments.

Doggie howled, and, without waiting for a command, sped through the dissolving gate and the evaporating daffodils, making for the sheep.

Which left Melba to draw her last, great breath, turning the storm without even trying.

She pushed it back from the safe land she'd soon inhabit with Doggie and Dad, and Jilly, if she ever managed to find her way.

For a moment that may have lasted a lifetime, she felt what it was like to hold her breath, and consider.

Only when she was ready to exhale did Melba erase the rotting carcass of the kangaroo, Mrs Palmer's prizewinning roses, and her own exhausted shell from the face of the earth.

WHEN THEIR MOTHERS made them friends, Frannie's mum was in her hippie phase, with a husband working for a bank in the city, and Mitch's mum was a divorced preschool teacher who'd recently returned to her career after having three kids.

The women met at the school fête, chatting in the long queue for fête food, kids dawdling either side. Frannie's mum suggested vegetarian rissoles, but Mitch and his siblings were set on hot dogs, which sparked a slightly defensive conversation about the mothers' different approaches to feeding their kids, but eventually softened into a coffee invitation and a play date.

And so Frannie showed Mitch their orchard and tumbledown outhouses. In the old timber shacks they made stories about being poor children living on a mountain in the distant past, a past they knew only from television shows.

Frannie and Mitch were always married in the game. Each had a younger sibling who never complained at being shoved in the shelves of a mouldy dresser for their beds, and Mitch had a quiet older sibling who was always the enemy. Too old for games, he lazed around the back steps and went to the toilet all the time.

Mitch knew why. Frannie's Dad kept his porn magazines in there. Discovered during their first visit, they showed naked women on rock ledges and sprawled over tree trunks. The elder boy was drawn to the anatomy he'd never seen in that light, while Mitch looked past the anatomy to the wanton looks on their faces, perplexed about what made them feel that way.

The two mothers knew what the regular toilet trips meant, and smiled that these boys were at the right stage at the right time.

Somehow, Frannie and Mitch's games did not translate to school, among the concreted in pine trees where the boys would swing on the lower branches, and the girls stuck to the hillside, skipping or playing hopscotch.

Mitch dawdled at the edge of the pines, never really joining in with either boys or girls. He wanted to try the rhythmic moves of hopscotch. It looked fun, but only for poofters. Jacks he could almost get away with because some of the other boys were drawn to its furtive suggestion of gambling.

But at Frannie's place, boys and girls could get away with playing the candle game. They all knew what that meant, and they all took their positions. The little ones were in the dresser, almost getting too big for it now. Frannie put a tablecloth around her head like she imagined a poor woman would, and went into the other room waiting for her cue.

Mitch took his place at the rickety table where the silver candlestick stood below a cob-webbed window.

Usually he'd spy his brother at this point, either loitering on the back steps or in the toilet, but on this particular day, Mum had let the older boy walk home by himself, hours ago.

So Mitch had to make sound effects for the Taxman, the part his brother always unwittingly played. They didn't know what a Taxman was, it just sounded bad the way the parents always spoke of it, someone who comes to the house and demands something from an innocent family.

When Frannie said: 'Ready ... go,' from behind the door, Mitch would pull the candle closer to the edge of the table where he had a pen and paper, and he'd imagine the pen was a fine feather quill and he was working out how much money their poor, poor family didn't have.

Then, he would rap on the bottom of the table, and the kids would shiver in the dresser and wail: 'The Taxman ... The Taxman Mummy'.

Frannie would come running to her children and calm them on her shoulder and put them back to bed, eyes deep with moisture, looking to Mitch for comfort, which he always gave with a hand on her shoulder, saying: 'I'll talk to him'.

But today Frannie didn't come when the kids trembled. Mitch knocked again, louder, and the kids trembled and cried louder again, laughing behind the doors of the crumbling furniture. When she didn't appear on the second cue, Mitch stood and went to the door.

'Frannie?' he called quietly.

'Come in,' she answered, under her breath.

He pushed the rotten timber door open and in the half light she swooped on him, elbows up like a bird, mouth closing on his so fast she had little time to get the words out.

'Let's *pash*,' she said, as she irreversibly changed the rules of the game.

MITCH and his siblings went up to the private school. There was a uniform to wear with a smart blazer jacket, and he looked the part, just like his brother, who'd quickly disappeared into the ranks of navy jackets and grey pants around different but familiar pine trees and arrangements of boys.

Frannie's mum teased Mitch's about 'all that money ... it's gotta come from somewhere,' and assumed that the rich mother was paying the fees. She also silently watched both boys change. Very soon neither of them came around for her baking (or the porn), and their mother came less and less.

Walking to school with his sister meant Mitch avoided most of the rowdiness and the name calling that school became for him. He wished he could disappear between classes, and fed himself on stories of wizards who could avoid all the pitfalls of high school on their magical adventures. Some of his teachers spotted the backwardness, but Mitch fitted right in with the Dungeons and Dragons crowd and got large enough fast enough to avoid being punched like the weedy kids.

He drew. It started on the corners of his exercise books, and soon became vast fantasies incorporating dragons, wizards, and here and there a warrior. No one thought anything of such images except that Mitch was getting very good at drawing. He worked harder on the warriors, fleshing them out from the far reaches of his imagination. If he disappeared between periods it was likely to be in the service of capturing a vast, broad and silent warrior on paper.

Everyone knew about the school disco from the notices that went up one Monday. Some year twelve students were given permission from the parents' auxiliary, and with the bar stocked only with soft drink, word spread to dress punk if you wanted to be cool.

Mitch's Mum was pleased at her second son's popularity with the girls by that year. 'Your harem,' she called them, 'you could pick any one of them anytime you want,' she encouraged him. Surely the disco night would prove too much for one of them and they'd jump him in the darkness outside, where the furtive smokers and drinkers would be hanging out.

So she opened her house to the kids to change into their punk costumes and do their hair with tins of coloured spray. The amount of girls coming over naturally attracted a few uninvited boys, but that didn't matter. Other young men were talking to her son, encouraging him to wear his hair in a high mohawk instead of the nerdy shock of wizard's locks he preferred.

She did chips and hot dogs to fill them up and get them out the door, and walked them to the highway, tousling coloured hair as they crossed, some of them already couples. There was a gaggle of girls around Mitch, one of them with her arm interestingly through his. She couldn't help but wink at her boy as he passed. He rolled his eyes, of course, and avoided her embrace.

The sports hall was a pulsating mass of dancers. A Madonna track filled every storeroom and cold cubicle with echoes of love and lust, fun and fantasy. Mitch stayed with his harem and they filled the edge of the dance floor close to the canteen, where befuddled parents blinked under fluorescent lights.

Their hands entwined but bodies separate, as the music changed to Duran Duran, most of the girls let out cries of approval and slipped away through the crowd.

Mitch lost no confidence alone. His height, and his mohawk, meant that most people did not recognise him. All they saw was a tall, angular, possibly handsome youth with a frozen face below bizarre hair, giving nothing away.

Someone let out a cry from behind him: 'He's such a spunk, let's go and dance near him,' and they shoved past Mitch towards the older kids who hogged the centre of the dance floor underneath the mirror ball and the streamers.

The spunk in question was Alan Putnick. Mitch had seen him naked in the change rooms at the school swimming carnival.

A crowd was drawn to him, but Alan danced alone. He was in leather, with a great sweep of hair he tossed around.

Mitch edged his way closer, his height carving a path, and raised both arms over his head to get close to Alan. They were almost the same height.

'Wild boys, never close their eyes,' the song went, 'Wild boys always ... *shine!*' and everyone held one another in unison, but Alan had his back to Mitch, and with a sweep of the gorgeous hair, he flung his body unwittingly against the younger boy.

The suddenness of intimacy was a delight and a shock. Mitch let go and Alan Putnick fell on top of him, twisting as he did so that Mitch was pressed face down onto the basketball lines, forced to exhale, and laugh.

Alan struggled, so uncool to not be in control. Then Mitch drew breath, inhaling aftershave in a long draught. Their faces met. For a moment Alan was confused, then a sneer so mean erased the joy from his face and Mitch retreated without question.

He dragged himself to his feet and drew back through the crowd, past the canteen, past the canoodlers in the shadows outside and the smokers on the oval, to the bush and the highway and all the way to his bed, where the shame of holding Alan Putnick's leather-clad ass could be made into a moment of pure joy and no shame.

FRANNIE caught the school bus from the end of the road by the old orchard to the state school three towns away.

She sought out the row of girls towards the back, the ones who sat in front of the boys. She'd heard these girls could show her how to stuff her bra with tissues.

'The boys go mad for it,' Kylie said, 'you watch,' and Frannie witnessed the row of senior boys ogling the girls getting off the bus out the front of the school, the way the languid, lanky older boy-men scuffed their shoes and checked out tits between strands of hair.

Frannie had a special book she wrote things in. It felt cool to stand aloof from the groups sometimes, pen dangling from her mouth, head at an angle, thinking deep thoughts and writing them down. It was different to the scrawls all the other girls wrote on their bags and their folders.

She put her thoughts together, mostly about boys and how one or two of them were not so pimply and not so weird, and might show a girl a thing or two in a big city somewhere, if only they could drive there alone or catch the train. The thwarting of their escape was always a part of Frannie's story.

Frannie found out about the party from a girl in year eleven. She only needed to work out an excuse for her mother, and how to get there, since it was three towns away.

The second problem was solved when Kylie said she'd make sure they picked her up. 'Just be on the corner of the highway by nine, and don't be late,' otherwise they'd leave her behind.

She thought about just asking her mum if she could go, but then there would be questions and probably an embarrassing lift there and back.

So she planted the seed in the form of a fake school project about possums, which of course were nocturnal. 'That means they only come out at night,' she announced firmly to her stupid younger sister within earshot of Dad.

He called her in, and tried to sit her on his lap. 'What's this about possums?' he asked, too close to her ear.

'I have to go and find some, for school,' she said. 'There's probably some in the bush by the corner, that block near the highway,' she added, starting to weave a thread which he picked up on.

Within minutes, he'd told Mum that Saturday night he and the girls were going possum spotting for Frannie's school project.

'She wants us to call her *Frances*, remember?' was all her mother said from her studio. She'd taken up ceramics.

Dad had already forgotten all about it the next day. By the weekend he'd be oblivious, and if she was caught out she'd simply say she went alone, 'because Dad forgot,' and all her mother's energy would be focussed on the errant father and not the daughter.

She nicked one of her mother's low cut tops. In the small bathroom of the old house, she perched on the toilet and pressed her arms underneath her breasts to make them bigger, and dropped her chin the way Kylie showed her.

Kylie said the car was a red Torana. Between the silence of the bush and the rush of the highway, Frannie realised she didn't know what a Torana looked like.

When the orange Cortina pulled slowly along the shoulder of the highway, Frannie knew her makeup would be running and was grateful of the dark back seat to hide her tears as she slid across the laps of three girls and a tall guy who complained as she manoeuvred across his lumpy crotch.

Three towns away they all piled into the house and the anonymity of the music. 'Love is a Battlefield' was blaring from the speakers on the verandah. Kylie disappeared quickly. The tall guy was from the Catholic school. He grinned at her as he slunk into the hallway, past the pashing couples by the door. Frannie followed him. To stay there, alone, under the gaze of the house, would have been unthinkable.

Inside was dim. There were sporty boys playing drinking games in the kitchen. She was drawn instead to a back room where kids were draped on sofas watching MTV.

Someone gave her a drink which tasted sweet, with a sting to her throat as she sipped it. There was a back verandah too. Smokers. Someone gave her one as she slid the door shut against the heat and the noise of the TV and the music. 'Thanks,' she said, leaning in for a light. An arm pressed down on her shoulders and stayed, steadying itself against her.

Something mixed into the fag too. She laughed at that, and kept laughing, then started coughing. The arm steadied her again, and someone patted her head and said: 'Awwww.'

Frannie giggled. The arm wasted no time. It leant on her more, cutting her off from the other smokers, and hot, moist lips closed on hers and she disappeared altogether. The tongue played with her, forced her down into the shadows by the deck. As she gasped for air, a sound misinterpreted as rising passion, she caught a glimpse of the Catholic school boy sneering as she was pulled into the garden shed under the house.

The last part, from the pash onwards, Frannie made up. The tall boy took another girl under the house, but in her mind, when she was under her doona with her secret book, she made him do it to her instead.

MITCH was on his way to the newspaper office to place an ad for a flatmate, and Frannie was window shopping outside the antique store. He noticed her faux leopardskin hat before he noticed it was Frannie wearing it. They laughed, went to shake hands, laughed again, then hugged.

He looked taller to her, still lanky, the way she remembered him in the private school uniform, and she said so.

He thought she looked smaller than ever. The hat seemed to swallow her up. He tried to avoid the question: 'So, what are you doing?' but it just slipped out.

'I'm a writer,' she said, reaching into her bag for fags before he could press her for further details. 'What about you?' she said, and closed her mouth around one.

'I'm an artist,' he said, watching her inhale, giving no more when no more was asked.

When she saw that their secrets were safe, she raved that she 'loved' being back home and was 'looking for someone to share a place with.'

He asked her to come and look at the room in his place, if she wanted.

She shrugged, said she probably would. They made a time.

Her friends, who owned a place around the corner, helped her move in that weekend. She had the front room in the weatherboard cottage, and he had the one at the back.

'Mum will be stoked,' she said, 'she's bringing my stuff up next week. You're sure it's okay for me to smoke in here?' she added.

'No problem,' he said, wishing he could have just said no.

She stubbed her cigarette out. 'I'll smoke on the front verandah. I can watch the world go by,' she laughed. He nodded and finished the washing up.

She watched him a moment, methodically placing the clean dishes on the rack, not stopping until everything was clean and dry.

Wow, she thought, *a man who cleans everything and dries it and puts it away. Mum will want us to set the wedding day.*

He'd be besotted, just like when they were kids, and he'd ask her to marry him and she'd say yes, even though there was nothing special about him, and she'd be pregnant by Christmas.

Hadn't there been that French woman when he was overseas studying art? He'd be ready for another woman by now. He owned the house too. His grandmother had died and left them all money. They'd laugh to their friends about how they said they'd be married when they were children, and how, twenty years later, it came true.

But when Frannie tried to net Mitch by showing him her porn collection, he came out to her.

He didn't have to say it, it was obvious the minute he took the magazine from her and lingered over the pages with naked men.

'I always knew you were a big *poof*,' she said (even though she'd been told in rehab to stop exaggerating). There was a silence, apart from their page turning, into which she said: 'Well, I'm an *alcoholic*.'

Mitch closed his magazine, and looked at her with sympathy.

'Aren't you going to say anything?' she asked.

'I'm just thinking Mum wouldn't be proud of me if I chucked you out for that,' he smiled.

'I go to meetings,' she blurted, 'I'm in rehab. My 'friends' around the corner is the halfway house. God Mitch, I needed to get this off my chest.'

'It doesn't matter,' he said, 'I hate pubs, and I was scared you'd be dragging me in all the time.'

'I'm done with all that now. I have another month of rehab, and I'm going to last this time. Living here is going to make it easier. I might even get back to my writing.'

She made them coffee, and Mitch got used to the idea that now one person in the world knew.

HE started going to a weekly gay support group for young men coming out. The young men were in their late teens, but Mitch was nearly thirty, and it made him feel even more pathetic.

He and Frannie joked about it, and called the group GayA, while she was attending AA.

Their collusion took place on the front verandah while she smoked, listing the fortunes of everyone they knew from school – who was a winner and who was a loser – but no one seemed to have ended up quite so unusual, quite so exotic, or quite so ripe with undiscovered potential as Frannie and Mitch, the alkie and the poofter.

At her 'dry discos' Frannie made it her personal mission to get Mitch a root, because he seemed to be a bit pathetic in that regard, but every guy she nodded towards, indicating *he's gay*, was either short or weird. The ones who made no secret of their interest were too old or too needy. Nobody had that special something he was looking for.

So he started going to the city, to the real clubs, where men came up and put their arms around him and no one gave a shit about snogging on the dance floor. He went home with any guy who was interested and bigger than him. Sometimes they were good lovers. Mostly they were useless. Mitch was still learning the difference, but at last he knew what made those women's faces the way they were in the porn magazine's at Frannie's all those years ago.

Frannie stayed at home and started cooking for herself again. First just mountains of mashed potato with piles of veggies, but then she got more adventurous and would plan three-course meals. Some of the rehab girls came around to keep her company, but mostly she missed Mitch.

Sometimes, out on the front verandah, she swore she could smell the pub fumes wafting down the street over her smoke. She imagined how easy it would be to drift through the door and sidle up to the first half decent man at the bar and dare him to buy her a drink.

She thought about writing. There was a novel in those rehab girls. *Rehab Girls* was a great title. She could see the cover design, and the book sitting on the bookshop shelves.

She thought of a story of an alkie chick who fell off the wagon by walking into the local pub, already drunk on the pub fumes.

Pub Fumes was also great title, and she could see the book cover, but the next cigarette always sucked the determination out of her, waiting for the sound of Mitch's loping footfalls coming down the pathway from the railway station.

WHEN he saw his grandfather's antique books spewed across the room, Mitch called the police. Small things had been nicked. Gems. Some of his gran's jewellery.

Frannie was due in at eleven after her shift at the café, but she wasn't there by the end of the next day. The café called looking for her. They hadn't seen her all yesterday and assumed she was sick. Mitch called her mother.

'She'll be down in the city,' came the jaded voice. 'It wasn't going to be forever,' she added. He tried to make a few rehab-like statements but she shrugged them all off. 'At least she doesn't have a key to this place. She's done *me* over more than once.'

The police didn't bother coming around, so Mitch passed the time by tidying the living room. He made dinner for himself and watched their favourite show.

By eight, he found himself on the train to the city. He checked every passing train for a sight of Frannie and her leopardskin hat, but the near-empty carriages held only strangers.

When he reached the last stop, he found himself seeking out the usual pathway to the sex clubs near the railway station, knowing he would find something beyond their neon stairwells.

More than once, he was asked if he wanted to accompany a man beyond a doorway. He declined, even when the offers came from men he liked the look of, using the falsely knowing bravado that he got straight from Frannie.

When he felt ready, he tried it on a guy who reminded him a little of Alan Putnick. There was the knowing smirk, the beckoning into the cubicle, and the coming together of bodies.

Mitch lowered himself onto the vinyl-covered bed, and went to lift his legs, but the guy had gone.

He sat up, alarmed, and hit the corridor again, in search of his errant lover, mouth and throat dry from the shock of the abandonment.

There, in a dark corner, he found his conquest with his arms working around another, younger boy. Before he could be spotted, Mitch retreated back into his clothes.

As he crossed the busy road outside, the vomit welled up inside him, and he ran into an alleyway where he sprayed his insides across sticky bricks, thinking if anyone saw him, he'd fit perfectly well into this sick, sad, suburb. When he was empty, he pissed his vomit off the wall, and wished he could call Frannie.

MITCH heard the whole story. Jed had only been a week out of rehab where the Drug Court had sent him instead of jail, and he'd started pocketing trinkets in Mitch's house only minutes after he took Frannie on the kitchen floor, her face pressed into the onion bag while he gave her such a pain-like pleasure throughout her body, the kind which she hadn't felt for years.

She couldn't stop him after that, just went with it. After Mitch's they shoplifted a service station, then headed for Cabramatta. He scored for them, and injected her first. He still had enough in his system from breakfast.

Frannie's face had pressed against the glass of the car window as she slid even deeper.

An hour later, Jed dropped her at a brothel.

She ran away from that one midweek, then worked another in

Parramatta to get the money for the train fare.

Standing at the front door, not feeling like she should use her key anymore, she knocked. A week on the run had stripped every ounce of fat from her. Mitch held her tight for a moment, then showed her in.

She could still see Jed's shape in the sheets, and wept.

'That bastard played me. All he wanted was a ride back to the city.'

'I'm not living with heroin,' Mitch said. It made her jaw drop.

'I'm not addicted to it ...'

'*I'm not living with heroin*,' Mitch boomed, 'do you understand me?'

His voice went through her like a blade. More pain, but she took it, and went for a bath. He cooked, fed her, and put her to bed, his bed.

THERE was a guy who Mitch knew was interested, very interested. He drove a hundred kilometres to see Mitch after they met at a bush dance. Before Mitch could get another look at his face and suggest they go for dinner, David had him on all fours in the hallway.

It was everything Mitch wanted, even a little hugging afterwards. That would increase, Mitch thought, when they did it in bed.

But they never did. Next time David lifted him onto the kitchen bench and grunted up against him, then left to see if his Mum had enough food in the house.

Mitch asked if he could come stay that weekend, but Dave said no, he was going away. When Mitch got huffy and wouldn't take his calls, Dave drove from the coast on Sunday night to have Mitch on the hallway floor again two minutes after walking through the door.

Frannie never managed to see this new flame. She was too busy going to NA meetings. 'He must be nice, but is he emotionally available?'

Mitch wanted to blurt out *of course he is*, but the question offended him. Dave was so cute. So rough and ready. Then the itching started a week after Dave called it off. Worse at night.

'You've got crabs,' Frannie said in front of the tele. 'Believe me, I know.'

The doctor asked Mitch a few unexpected questions about his sex life, so he gave himself up for the full round of tests.

When they called to tell him to come in for the results, he forgot about the appointment and they had to call again, Frannie took the message.

'Get yourself in there,' she warned. 'Believe me. I know.'

The female doctor brought the file in, tapped it on her hand, and said: 'Your test results show that you're HIV negative.'

She reeled off the need for a second test in three months to confirm, mentioned a course of antibiotics for the throat gonorrhea, some cream for the crabs and signed him a script for all of it, said to come in next week for more tests and did he have any questions?

Frannie made him his dinner and put him to bed. Her bed.

SHE met Fred at a dry disco.

'How long have you got up?' she asked, blowing her cigarette smoke onto him, trying to give him the not interested vibe.

'Aw, I'm not ... you know ... I'm not,' he mumbled.

'You mean you could have a drink, but you're choosing not to?'

'Yeah, that's it,' he said.

'Well, fuck you then,' she said, and headed back inside.

Fred proved persistent. He began to pay visits, finding Frannie smoking on the balcony and Mitch sunning himself.

'He's a gentleman,' Mitch said, 'it takes guts to turn up here knowing we're watching and talking about him. Anyway he's cute.'

'But I haven't told him yet,' she said.

'You think he doesn't know you're an addict? How long have you been clean this time?' Mitch asked.

'Nine months and two weeks tomorrow,' she replied.

Fred stayed when he heard about the booze. When he heard about the heroin, he skipped a beat, was slightly browned-off when he dropped her home, but after sleeping on it and calling her in the morning, he stayed. She never told him about the brothels.

The only thing that really worried Fred was Mitch.

He told Frannie at the local Chinese, and she laughed. 'He's gay, you realised that, you big idiot!'

'Yeah, I know that,' Fred said, 'but doesn't he ever, you know, take a wrong turn on his way back from the dunny and sleep in the wrong bed?'

'What?' Frannie exclaimed, 'Mitch? No way. He likes men. You might be his type, so watch out.'

'What's my type then?' Fred asked, bringing her back to life, the way he liked her.

'All muscles and no brain.'

He laughed, and asked her to move in with him. She said yes, and he ordered dessert for them both.

MITCH met Mark at an HIV-AIDS fundraiser, hosted by the pub he and Frannie avoided. Mark asked him to dance, the first time a man had ever done that, and it was not just awkward individual dancing Mark wanted from Mitch, he held Mitch by both hands, and they carved a path through the drag queens and the teenagers, moving at their own pace.

Mark was slightly taller, with a deep voice. He was almost too good to be true, an accountant with a local firm, and Mitch had spied him coming and going from the clinic.

Which meant either this man was a complete slut with every STD known to mankind, or he was HIV positive.

Mark drove Mitch home that night. They chatted in the car for half an hour. Mitch almost asked him inside, but Mark waved and drove off. Not a slut, then.

Flowers delivered the next day, and dinner out the next weekend.

Frannie was impressed. 'Your mum will like this one, you should take him around soon. Get it over with.'

Mitch thought not. He rarely saw Mum these days. She'd met a man after fifteen years of celibacy.

Paul, a real estate agent, was shorter than her, with weird taste in casual clothes.

Mitch found himself telling all this to Mark. He could never seem to shut up, reeling off his whole life, holding the other man's hands under restaurant tables, hands like bunches of bananas, hands Mitch could rest against.

They had nearly ten dates before Mark made his move.

He drove Mitch to his place, kissed him passionately up the stairs, made love to him in his bedroom and hugged him until morning.

Mitch was besotted, desolate to leave the presence of this large angel, even for a minute.

FRANNIE knew she was pregnant when her usually traumatic period was late, and took her test results to Fred's work at the phone company.

'Won't have to get off the booze for the baby,' he joked, hugging her to him like a vice. There was celebration from the city to the bush that Fred had finally reproduced.

When he heard, Mitch tried to call her, but they'd gone away for the weekend.

Mark said: 'Great news for a pair of breeders,' and, 'hope they stop at one. Best thing for the environment.'

Mitch called Frannie again in the week but no one answered. He and Mark went away to the coast the next weekend, and the weekend after that they had dinner with a lawyer friend of Mark's and his boyfriend. By the time Mitch caught up with Frannie, she was in her second trimester.

'IT'S just more tests,' Mark complained, using the tone he always used when he just wanted Mitch to shut up and change the subject.

'Then why didn't you tell me?' Mitch wailed.

'Because it's nothing. It always is. You know how it is, they call you in to tell you the results because they can't tell you on the phone,' Mark explained, trying to do his tie in a hurry and get out the door.

'How much blood did they take?' Mitch fired.

'I don't know. I never look.'

'How many vials were on the desk afterwards?'

'The usual. I don't know.'

'I'm coming with you,' Mitch decided out loud from the bathroom.

'I don't want you to worry about it, it's nothing.'

'If they want to check the drug therapies are as effective as they could be, you might have to change meds,' Mitch said.

Mark rolled his eyes, but Mitch wasn't convinced. He waited at the clinic until Mark showed up, went in with him, and held his hand in the waiting room. They had a giggle at the sexually transmitted diseases brochures, lined up alphabetically, and smiled at Doctor Sharon Yang, who greeted them and said: 'Mark, Mitch. So you two are together now? Lovely. Come in.'

Dr Sharon was heavily pregnant, which they joked about, but she waved off their offers of pulling out chairs and holding the door.

'There's some abnormality in the results,' she said, still smiling, 'but what concerns us more is the drop in T-cells over the last few tests.'

'Going back how long?' Mitch asked.

'Steadily decreasing for at least six months,' Sharon added, flicking a pen. 'There's a new combination therapy available we want to start you on, straight away. There are side effects.'

'Here we go,' Mark said, 'the old side effects.'

The diarrhea and high temperatures started within forty-eight hours. Mitch called Mark's work and got him three days off before he'd need a medical certificate.

Mark groaned with every T-cell saved by the drugs coursing through his veins. Sharon made a house call, said the high temperature was normal. If it subsided in under a week, then it was going to work.

When it didn't, Mark's skin went grey. On the next house call, Sharon called a halt to it.

'It doesn't work for everyone,' she said, looking about the room for a place to sit with a large belly, frustrated at her failure, lines of sweat coursing down her temples.

Mitch cleared a chair for her and she sat without letting go of Mark's hand. 'We can put you back on your old meds and see if that makes a difference,' she said, unsure. 'I like your house Mark, did you do the colour scheme yourself?'

Mark nodded, hardly there, yet managing a smile. Sharon smiled in return. 'You call me, even if it's late,' she whispered to Mitch as she left.

Mitch sat by his man, cleaning his sweaty skin while he dozed. He'd seen photos of Mark as a child, sunny country town snaps. Never before had his angel looked so childlike, caught between clammy sheets.

The house was a mess, signs of struggle from one end to the other, a battle with blood and resistance, of bold attempts to shore up immunity, the enemy coursing deep and heavy beneath Mark's translucent skin.

After sleeping a while beside one another, Mark woke. His eyes were not so milky. He let Mitch wrap his head in soft hands, and they whispered to one another that *it was going to be okay.* Mitch kissed his face, assuring, and settled his frame in beside Mark's for the night.

AN hour after Frannie went into labour, Fred called Mitch and asked him to come to the maternity ward. They watched Frannie's long-held boast of a drug-free birth disappear when one of the nurses just starting the evening shift mentioned the word 'epidural', hoping for a quiet night.

After six hours of the most intense pain she'd ever felt, Frannie shakily agreed, and half an hour after the syringe, she was sitting up in bed drinking a cup of tea.

By nine in the evening the baby's heart rate showed distress. By nine thirty the word 'caesarian' was mentioned, and by ten Frannie was rushed into surgery and the baby was wrenched from her stomach.

'At least my pelvic floor is intact,' she joked as the drugs they used to wake her kicked in, a bit sore but flushed with delight at the little boy they'd called Roman.

MARK didn't tell his firm why he left. To cope with the lack of income, he moved into Mitch's place.

He spent his days out of suits and in loose clothing which allowed the warm breezes of the coming summer to bring his skin back to life. Mitch got a job at the regional gallery and used Mark's car to commute four days a week.

At night, as they lay in bed, their bodies joined deeper than the same time last year. Mark's three-day growth rested against Mitch's downy blond neck, and they spoke more gently to one another than they ever had ever done before.

FRANNIE had gotten into the habit of making Fred wear condoms, but he forgot to bring them to the coast, and didn't feel like running down to the service station with a hard on in his pants, so they just did it.

She knew what to expect this time, although she was not one of those determined mothers who would try for a natural birth after having a C-section.

Compared to her sister, Frannie decided, she still looked hot, with none of that extra bulk around the hips that came from everything having been pushed aside when the child came out. A Caesarian also meant Frannie could legitimately take drugs and no one could stop her.

The large purple envelope came with a stack of bills, which she left for Fred. She ripped it open. A square card, silver-edged, inviting them both to celebrate the wedding of Mitchell and Mark.

'Why do they have to get married?' her Mum said on the phone, minutes later, 'it's not as though it's legal or anything.'

'Mum,' Frannie huffed, thinking similar thoughts, 'I think it's lovely. Mitch needs someone too.'

'Kind of weird though,' her Mum said, already sounding distant and annoyed at having been called away from her paper making.

'So you definitely haven't been invited?' Frannie asked.

'I thought the fellow was sick anyway?'

'He's a lot better now. I saw them a few weeks ago and he was through the worst of it, they said.'

A few weeks ago was in truth nearly three months. The news made her obtuse, like her day had been spoiled. She cancelled her appointment with the doctor and made it for next week, just to be sure her period was not about to happen. She'd call Mitch that night.

Mitch called her at the end of the week. She pretended not to have checked the post box, making excuses about Roman being a bit off colour.

'It's great news Mitch,' she said, 'I'm very happy for you.'

'What about I come around this weekend?' he suggested.

'This weekend? Can I check with Fred and call you back?'

'No worries,' Mitch said.

'No worries, okay, see you then, hopefully. If we don't connect then, we will soon.'

'Okay Frannie,' Mitch said, his hand already putting the receiver down.

A MONTH after the invitations went out, Mitch got home from work to an empty house, no sign of Mark. He called around a few friends, but no one had seen him.

As night fell he got the call from the hospital. Mark was in intensive care.

'Who did you say you were?' the triage nurse asked Mitch from behind the glass barrier.

'Mark's partner,' Mitch blurted.

'The family didn't mention anyone else,' she said, looking at Mark's file, 'they're in there now.'

'Let me in please, someone from here rang me,' Mitch pleaded.

'I can't, I'm sorry. You have a different surname.'

'How is Mark? What's happened?'

'I cannot just give out details, perhaps if I ask the mother?'

I don't know her. She doesn't know me. She won't know me, Mitch thought as the woman disappeared. He could see her blurry form in the corridor beyond, through the scratched and milky perspex. He also saw the tall form of a man with a hat. The nurse reappeared, no change in her demeanour.

'The family has asked that you come back tomorrow.'

'Tomorrow?'

'Yes, tomorrow,' and she sat back down and indicated that he should go.

Mitch called Doctor Sharon.

Fifteen minutes later, she pulled into the emergency driveway, took her little girl from a car seat in the back, and, with her spare hand, took Mitch by the hand, only letting go for the short time it took to open the triage security door with the pass card around her neck.

'There will be a complaint about this treatment,' was all she said to the nurse, who did not turn around.

Inside, they looked left and right, where light shone from between drawn curtains.

'Where is Mark Simpson?' Sharon called, summoning a nurse.

'Number five,' someone called, and pulled aside the grey divider.

There he was, off-colour, breathing through a mask. A stoney-faced man rising up into a hat and a woman clutching her handbag stood at one side, and a very young doctor at the other.

Sharon moved first and nestled her little girl in the crook of Mark's arm.

'Hi Mark, what's happened?' she asked, reaching for his chart.

'I'm his doctor,' she said. The other doctor muttered a few details and disappeared.

'All this fuss, about nothing,' Mark said.

'I see you forgot to update your emergency contact information, silly man,' Sharon said, before looking at his parents. 'Mr and Mrs Simpson, lovely to meet you, I am Sharon, you've come a long way.'

'Mum, Dad, this is Mitch,' Mark said. Neither of them changed the expressions on their faces. Neither extended a hand, although Mitch did without even thinking. No one allowed space for him to sidle up and kiss Mark.

'Is he going to be alright?' Mr Simpson said.

'Oh, I should think so. We're still getting his medication right, you see, it's trial and error, hopefully not too much error,' Sharon said.

The mother rolled her eyes, it was the only movement in the cubicle.

Sharon looked for some recognition in the parents, but could find none. Years of experience taught her to know when she'd been clear enough with a family, so she replaced Mark's chart and smiled at the two men she knew so well.

'I'll go speak to my colleague about you, and come check on you in the morning. Come to mummy?' she called, stretching her arms out to her little one, who complied. 'Give Mark a kiss,' Sharon said, and the little girl found a patch of skin on the side of his jaw, where the mask did not cover him, then she smiled into her hand at all the silent adults.

'Night-night precious,' Mark said, a whisper through the mask.

The father shut the curtain behind the doctor. 'Open it Dad,' Mark said.

'Best way to catch something in a hospital, leaving the door open,' the older man said. 'I don't like that doctor. Anyway, we've got to find somewhere to stay, if we're going to stay.'

'You can stay at ours,' Mitch said, 'we have a spare room, if you'll just let me go ahead and get it ready.'

'Oh no,' the mother said, 'there's a motel across the highway.'

'We'll be leaving early tomorrow,' her husband said, as though it were an explanation.

They were gone in minutes. The closest either of them got was Mark's mother patting the blanket near her son's knee. Mark shrugged, his disappointment welling from his gut, and kissed Mitch.

'You don't want them annoying you around the place. He farts constantly and she'll clean the toilet about five times an hour,' he laughed, patting his man on the shoulder.

They lay together, the curtains drawn against the florescent lights, the only sound was the slight wheeze of the oxygen as it was forced deeper into Mark's system than he was capable of doing for himself.

When Mitch got home he called Frannie to let her know, but got Fred.

'Mate, she's gone to a meeting,' Fred told Mitch down the line, as he looked at Frannie across the kitchen.

FRANNIE was heavily pregnant by the time the wedding happened. Unhappily big this time, she found nothing comfortable or totally hot to wear. All pretensions of being a yummy mummy went out the window. Her mum agreed to mind Roman.

Fred couldn't make the actual ceremony because of work, but would be there about an hour later. Frannie knew he was just making it up, but couldn't bring herself to say she wished she had an excuse too.

She arrived earlier than she'd hoped and got stuck chatting with Mitch's mum, who was nervous, jaded, looking older than she was and flirty all at once.

She made a point of handing Frannie between people who all mauled at her great stomach, and got stuck in a low modular lounge on the side verandah which Mitch's mum assured would give her a great view.

Seated next to her was Paul, Mitch's Mum's new partner, squashed into the corner of the lounge because, to him, it seemed safer than getting anywhere near the action of a gay wedding.

Frannie latched herself onto him. It seemed safer than standing out on the edge of everything.

When the boys arrived, Frannie forgot herself for a moment, because they both looked so gorgeous and so well.

There was a great cheer when Mark and Mitch pledged themselves to one another. Frannie couldn't see from where she was sitting. She only caught glimpses of faces, few of whom she recognised.

People went for booze at the makeshift bar in Mitch's studio.

Fred arrived and tried to cheer her up. The fact that he had almost downed a beer before he kissed her made sure she wasn't going to have a good time.

No dancing, no laughing, no wedding cake and, after only half an hour she demanded they leave without saying goodbye

FRED bought her a laptop when Flynn was born, and she was uploading all his first photos onto Facebook, wondering if she had enough time to do it before Mitch and Mark came around.

There was a Caesarian mothers' group on there, and Frannie spent hours sharing stories with other mothers about her experience.

Most of the time, though, the other women's stories bored her, and she'd already started blocking comments from anyone who tried to suggest she wasn't really interested.

She was going to show all those Facebook bitches by starting a mummy blog.

But she couldn't settle to it. She made another coffee and had another piece of toast.

She was hornier now than ever, and Fred usually obliged, but that morning he'd turned Frannie down, just stumbled out of bed with a limp dick. She hated the picture of it, hanging in her mind.

Suddenly she didn't want to see her old friend. Not ever again.

The anger inside her welled up so strongly that she stood, crossed the room past the new kitchen benches that she had to admit were already starting to look a little shabby, and was about to look up the train times to Cabramatta.

All that fucking free time they must have, without kids, she thought.

She wanted the silence of sliding down the inside of a car window as the hit ran through her, and wondered if Roman was old enough to tell his father what he had seen, if she went, and if she decided to take them with her.

So she texted Mitch.

When there was no reply after two texts, she put the baby to bed, shut all the blinds, gave Roman a dose of that cough mixture that sent him to sleep, and turned on *Doctor Phil*.

They were talking to women who'd had their tubes tied but were having the procedure reversed after their husbands had found out.

For a moment, Frannie forgot herself. The stupid cow who was crying in the chair next to Doctor Phil looked as though she deserved everything she got.

She went for another coffee and got out the packet of pop tarts she'd hidden in the laundry.

If the boys turned up, she'd just flick off the tele and stay quiet, and if Mitch was stupid enough to say anything about it later, she'd just say she forgot, because she needed to go to a meeting. If that didn't work, there was always screaming and tears.

'MITCH?' Frannie said from the other side of her bed.

'Yeah?' he answered.

'If I get crabs from this, I won't mind.'

'Okay,' he replied, still mortified at the prospect of having to wash all their clothes and sheets because of something he'd picked up from a man who behaved like a stray dog.

'We can just wash everything in the morning, and you can share your Lysol with me, okay?'

'Okay Frannie,' he said, turning to face the flannel pyjamas across her small back.

'Lysol doesn't hurt or anything,' she said, 'but you have to put it on your whole body, everywhere.'

They listened to one another breathing for a few minutes, then she said: 'Mitch?'

'Yeah?' he replied.

'You ever thought about having kids?'

'People always told me that I would make a good father,' he said into the darkness, which erased their whole past and concealed their entire future, just for a night.

'It was only because I played with my own dolls. It was their way of assimilating my sexuality, before I even knew what my sexuality was.'

'Cut the psychobabble Mitch, did you ever want to? Do you ever want to?'

'I don't know,' he said, 'maybe?'

'Well, if you ever do, I'll give you an egg, and you can rent my uterus. I won't ever manage to keep a guy long enough to have kids anyway.'

'Thanks,' he laughed.

'We don't have to have it off, but we could, if we wanted to.'

'Thanks Frannie,' he murmured.

She seemed to agree, to make a sound in reply. Whether it was just her descent into sleep, or that what she'd said was a deal, he was never really sure.

A Quick Fix

TO: dadandmum1067@hotmail.com

FROM: libbyloo22@hotmail.com

RE: Hi from school

DATE: August 27th 2015

Dear Daddy,

This is going to be a really, really long email because I have so much to say after your email last week. I can hardly remember all my questions, there are just so many. It was so nice to see you and Mummy at school on Family Day. Fiona and Becka think you look like an actor off an American TV show, one of the detective ones. They get to watch it in the school holidays. I just shrugged because I didn't know what they were talking about, but you can probably be flattered by the comparison and not at all offended, the way they were going on about it, okay?

I think I understand most of your email, and I am glad you wrote. You and Mummy looked so sad (or something) before you left. I knew you'd had a bit of a shock because of Uncle Tim being there.

It was the school counsellor who suggested I invite Uncle Tim to Family Day. She also said I should tell you first, but I didn't, and I am truly sorry for that, but I hope you will understand that I knew you'd say no or get upset and I wouldn't get to see you and Mummy properly on that day either. It's such a long time until the end of term and we have all the exams before that and I wanted to see my Daddy and Mummy.

I don't want you to be angry at the school counsellor. She's not one of those ferals or anything, and I want you to go easy on her if you complain. I told her about Uncle Tim last year, because of something we'd been reading at school. I'm not going to tell you what it was so you can't complain about it, okay? Something in it made me think about what you and Mummy told us about Uncle Tim, and I asked the counsellor to help me understand it. She took me aside and we talked it through, and now I understand better than I did before about Uncle Tim.

She told me something similar to what you said last year, and I want you to know I understand what you say, but I still don't think that means we can't see Uncle Tim. It's not fair really. That's why I rang him and asked him to Family Day.

I didn't think he'd come. I didn't think he'd even want to talk to me. He was very calm. The counsellor said he might be angry and that he might hang up on me, or be rude and aggressive. But he was nothing like that. He said it was a pleasant surprise to hear from me, and asked how I was doing at school, and was glad to hear I was doing English Extension because he liked English at school too. He asked me if we'd done *Pride and Prejudice* yet and I told him we had and we laughed about Mr D'Arcy and how the girls were all so silly about him. Uncle Tim said he always thought Mr Wickham sounded like much more of a catch. I have to say that gave me a bit of a shock, but I just laughed. Uncle Tim laughed too. There was a bit of an awkward pause, then Uncle Tim asked me if you and Mummy had told me about him and his lifestyle. I said yes, we knew about it. He asked me if it mattered that he was the kind of man who liked Mr Wickham instead of Lizzie Bennet, and I said that I didn't think it mattered much. Uncle Tim then asked me if I was sure I knew what you and Mummy meant. His voice was a bit wobbly, like he was getting a bit upset. I asked him if he was upset, and he just said he was relieved more than anything else.

I got his email address and we've been emailing a lot since, so when Family Day came up again this year I thought I'd ask him to come along. Please don't get angry reading this Daddy. Please take some time before you just get angry again.

The school counsellor said that Uncle Tim might have a special friend who might like to come too. I asked Uncle Tim and he said no, his special friend (who is called Matt) was not going to come to Family Day. He might come next year, but Uncle Tim seemed to think it best if only he came along the first time. He said you and Mummy have never met Matt. Is that right Daddy?

Kylie dared me to ask if Uncle Tim and Matt were going in the Mardi Gras parade, but I didn't want to ask anything like that. Kylie has a cousin who's a woman who has a special friend who's a woman, and none of her family ever see them. The only thing any of the family know about them is that they both have short hair. One of them works for the Council. Sarah said she probably drives trucks, but Sarah just likes to get the attention.

I tried to make it that you, Mummy and Uncle Tim weren't going to have to see much of each other on Family Day. That's why I asked you and Mummy to come at lunch and not earlier. I know you wondered why I asked you that, and I couldn't tell you why, but I never told you a lie about it, did I? I asked Uncle Tim to the morning tea and he thought that sounded splendid and that he'd wear his best tie. When I told him it was on a terrace he guessed there'd be wisteria or something, and I said the magnolias were coming into flower then. He said he'd get me to put one on his lapel. You saw it there, I know. I noticed you looking at it.

Daddy, you weren't supposed to meet Uncle Tim on the terrace. I wanted you all to meet at the lunch when there were more people around and I could be sure you'd all behave yourselves. The counsellor agreed with me on that point. But when I saw you and Mummy walking up the front steps my heart sank, because I could see it was all going to be a disaster and that you hadn't listened to me when I needed you to. You didn't give me time to explain to you and Mummy in private about what was happening, and I am still a bit angry about that. I hope I will get over it soon though.

I thought Uncle Tim was very polite in the circumstances. He left us alone for a while and got us all a cup of tea and some of the nicest cakes, and talked with some of the other parents while we had our first talk about it. I'm glad you didn't blow your top Daddy, but I do think you might have shaken Uncle Tim's hand when he offered it to you. When you think about it, there was no one on the terrace who could have told that Uncle Tim is a homosexual, just by looking. He was wearing a suit just like yours, and he was quite comfortable talking with the other adults. I saw him talk to the Headmistress for a long time and she seemed quite at ease with him, and Mr and Mrs Banks wanted him to sit with them at lunch because they found him so entertaining.

I suppose Uncle Tim should have taken them up on their offer because lunch with us was no fun for him. I didn't think it was fun either. You and Mummy didn't make much of an effort to ask about Uncle Tim, and I know the last time you saw him was at my christening. A lot can happen in fifteen years. To just sit there, ignoring his questions, was so embarrassing Daddy. Your face was very red and Mummy looked as though she was going to cry. Even when the Bankses came up with Fiona you still didn't lighten up. Can you blame Uncle Tim for excusing himself and having his coffee with them instead of us?

I saw Uncle Tim for a minute before he left. It was when I went to the toilet. I was crying and I could see he had been. He said perhaps we'd made a mistake, and gave me a little hug. Mrs Taylor our English teacher was coming out of the Ladies and I introduced her to Uncle Tim. She said it must be very pleasant to have my Uncle here. I said yes, and had a little more of a cry, and he gave me another hug. Uncle Tim said to Mrs Taylor we were having a few family issues, and that the school counsellor was aware of them, and that I was going to be okay in a little while, and I was.

Mrs Taylor patted Uncle Tim on the shoulder and said he was a very good man to be so caring of his niece. He nodded, and he was gone in ten minutes, saying he thought it was best, and that he'd be in touch soon, and I wasn't to stay upset, but to have a great afternoon and he'd come and see me in another piece of drama another time. He didn't want me to be upset and forget my lines or anything.

He gave me a present then, and I am not giving it back. It's too lovely Daddy. I'm not telling you what it is. I'm doing this because I know you told me a lie when you said Uncle Tim couldn't even pay you and Mummy the courtesy of saying goodbye. You thought I was in the toilet, but I was watching you, and you were so angry you didn't even turn your back to say goodbye to Uncle Tim. Mummy looked at him and nodded, but you didn't say anything. I think he was crying a little when he left. The Bankses tried to get him to come with them. I think they could see why, but he very politely excused himself, saying he needed to be at work for the afternoon.

I had to go and get ready for *Romeo and Juliet*. I know you sent Mummy with me so you could go and get angry at the counsellor. She's there so we can tell her things we need to tell her. Things that we can't say to other people, even our parents. She never said a word about what you'd said to her, just that I should try to understand your response too, and that is why I am writing, to let you know I am trying to understand.

Romeo and Juliet wasn't as fun as I'd hoped it would be, not after the lunch we'd had. Mummy was supposed to help me with my hair, but she had half an eye on where you'd got to and I needed to ask Mrs Simms to put my hair up for me. Mummy made no secret of the fact that she wished I was in a dress and not dressed up as the Apothecary. Mrs Taylor could see how disappointed Mummy was about that, but Kylie played Macbeth last year and it was her turn to play one of the female parts and as Mrs Taylor told us all at the last rehearsal that the Apothecary plays a major role in the tragedy, being the one who gives Romeo the draught to make him sleep and appear dead.

And anyway all the roles were played by men when they were first performed, even in front of Kings and Queens of England, so there should be no problem for girls in our class to dress as men. It's a girls' school Daddy, you know that.

I think Mummy was just not herself after seeing Uncle Tim. Uncle Tim said he thought it might have something to do with an idea you and Mummy might have about homosexual people dressing up like the opposite sex? I don't know. I was too upset by then to care and I fluffed most of my lines and you didn't see any of it anyway because you were busy with the counsellor and the day was over by then anyway.

When I said that I didn't want us to sit down with the counsellor that afternoon I meant it because I was too upset. You were angry and just wanted one of your quick fixes, but Daddy I honestly think, from the bottom of my heart, that this is something that cannot benefit from one of your quick fixes. I know you've had some success at Church with your quick fixes, but somehow I think it was best just to leave the day as it was and for you and Mummy to go home and for me to eat my dinner by myself so I could think. I know you were shocked when I said that so strongly, but I meant it. I gave you a kiss and a hug and I meant those too. I love you Daddy, you know that, but right then I was so stirred up I couldn't sit down anywhere.

I went for a long walk around the oval. Kylie found me when she'd said goodbye to her parents, and we walked and walked. She thought Uncle Tim was charming, and we made it like a scene out of *Pride and Prejudice* and that got my sense of humour back and I half hoped you and Mummy would still be there when we got back, but you'd gone and I don't blame you. I ate with my home room class, some of whom have no parents, or ones that couldn't come, and that made me feel very grateful to have a family at all.

A few days later I got your email. We don't get much time in the internet room, so it took me two sessions to read it and I had to get permission to print it out so I could look at it on my dorm. I can see you've thought very long and hard about it all, but it's too complicated for just one of your talks and a session with the Bible. Without you here to guide me I had to set it all up for myself and read the section you're talking about, and that took me the rest of the week because we had a lot of homework and the exams coming up.

It's clear from the bits you quoted from Leviticus that you think Uncle Tim is an abomination. I had to look that word up in the dictionary. In my dictionary, it says this – 'Something or someone that causes great revulsion or abhorrence.' I then had to look up the word 'abhorrence' and found this: 'Disgusting, loathsome, repellant. In opposition; completely contrary.' I then had to look up the word 'contrary' and found this: 'Opposed, as in character or purpose; completely different.'

Please follow me on this Daddy, because I am trying to show you how I really, truly feel deep down about what you wrote. Yes, in Leviticus chapter 18, verse 22 it says: 'Thou shalt not lie with mankind, as with womankind: it is abomination.' I know you were worried that I would not understand what 'lie down with' means, but as Mummy told you we have had our sex education classes last year, and I kind of know what it all means. I think there is a lot more to know.

Anyway, back to the point, and that is this – by following the meaning of the words, from 'abomination' we get the meaning 'different', and that is all. Do you see what I am getting at Daddy? Uncle Tim might lie down with a man, which is just different to what you might want to do, different in purpose. Do you see what I am getting at?

I read some of the other chapters of Leviticus, and looked it up on the internet. I asked permission for this from the internet room prefect and she watched me while I did it. Here is what I found interesting.

It says: 'Leviticus contains laws and priestly rituals, but in a wider sense is about the working out of God's Covenant with Israel set out in Genesis and Exodus – what is seen in the Torah as the consequences of entering into a special relationship with God (specifically Yahweh). These consequences are set out in terms of community relationships and behaviour.'

And from this I see that Uncle Tim just does not want a special relationship with God. But this does not mean we shouldn't speak to him, or that I shouldn't have asked him to Family Day, or that you and Mummy shouldn't be civil to him if you see him somewhere, even unexpectedly. I would be very surprised if you said that was true Daddy, that you could sit me down in front of me and tell me that if Uncle Tim has a 'different purpose' to you that we shouldn't talk to him or know what he's up to in his life.

After all, Mummy didn't take a lamb to be sacrificed a year after I was born, did she? And you have shaved your sideburns off, and we all like seafood when we go to the coast, and if we stuck to what it says in Leviticus, we'd have to be watching all that, and you'd only have a right to take one slave girl, and no more. We don't have slaves nowadays Daddy.

Before you blame anyone for this you must blame Mummy first, because it was she who told me I even had an Uncle.

There is a photo of the two of you together in an album she got out the day we couldn't go to the zoo because it was raining. You were both in your school uniforms (and you both had some pretty big sideburns!), and I asked who was that friend of yours you had your arm around, and didn't he look like Daddy? Mummy looked at the photo a bit closer. I think she was a bit confused about which of you was which. She said you were the one on the left and Uncle Tim was the one on the right.

I asked her who Uncle Tim was, and she said to ask you. You never would tell me, and Kylie found him on Facebook because she is allowed to use Facebook at home when she's on holidays.

Please forgive me Daddy, and try to understand. One more thing to help you, and I hope it is a quick fix. I found it in Leviticus 19 verse 17: 'Thou shalt not hate thy brother in thine heart.'

Lots of love,

Your Libby xoxoxox

WALLY TAYLOR'S GRANDDAD lived in the good room at the front of the farmhouse, with a photograph of Nanna above his bed so he didn't have to see it.

A tall, sharp shadow of a man who always stood high over the landscape of the farm, he was deeply burnished, despite his skin always being covered from neck to ankle in dark suits and a broad hat from which only the tip of his grey beard appeared in the full sun.

The kids stood still whenever they saw his shadow approach, no matter what they were doing. Any shouting or laughing had to be done a long way from the verandah, or out he'd come and bark: 'Shut it all up!' which would set the dogs off and make Mum frown.

Not that Wally noticed if Mum frowned. His little sister noticed though. Alice would be called to her Mother's apron, the same way Mum called for the older dogs and clucked for the chooks to come get their scraps.

Wally never saw any of that. If Granddad appeared on the porch Wally would leg it to the other side of the sheep yards and chuck stones at the windmill. The stones were really lumps of soil. They'd shatter to dust when they connected with the metal ribs of the rusted iron.

One day, after Alice was called and Wally patted Mickey, one of the old dogs, panting under his arm in the shade of the shearing shed, he spied Granddad's shadow striding up the hill behind the house. His legs were hidden by sandy-coloured grass, dried from luscious green into the straw that pelted the sun back under the brim of your hat and into your eyes. Wally sprinted after the dark form.

Granddad made no acknowledgement of him as they panted up the hill, leaning on a spade which nicked the earth every few steps, leaving a black cut, the dark loam spraying in an arc behind them.

There was no yelling at Wally, no: 'Get away from it', so the man and boy and dog continued in a line up the hill.

At the top, Mickey spied a rabbit and went for it after checking with the old man first. Just the merest flick of a finger was enough permission, and they watched as Mickey went in a wide arc and had the bunny in his mouth before it knew it was being pursued.

Granddad turned and looked back at the house, so far down you could see more roof than anything, the iron bouncing the sun away to the right towards the bend of the river.

The old man spat at Wally's feet. The saliva dried almost instantly. He swept his gaze northwest to the low blue hills, clocking the passage of clouds, which might have rolled through from that direction in a better year. To the south he spied the little town at the crossroads, and pointed for the boy.

'They'll see our tree from there,' he growled, 'and everyone will know the way to the Taylor's land,' and before Wally could descry the spire of the church where he went to Sunday School, the old man assaulted the earth with the spade.

'Which tree, Granddad?' Wally asked as they both looked at the hole. There was a brush of a hand at his neck. Wally flinched, thinking it was going to be a clip around the ear, but a hand rested on his shoulder and spun him around towards the west. There was a hessian bag, and tied in it a strange little tree, taller than Wally but not much.

Granddad lugged the tree over, tugged it out of the bag and into the hole, soil sluicing between his aged fingers as he pressed the wound back between folds of stubbly grass.

'You make a well, like this,' Granddad said, heaping soil on the downhill side, 'to hold whatever water comes.'

'Can I do the watering? Can I do the watering?' Wally jumped, but a hand pressed him back to earth. Granddad was looking to the southwest, and a light wind flicked the brim of his hat up a little, so Wally could see the squint of Granddad's eyes as the old man sought any trace of cloud.

'Might be a little rain tonight,' Granddad whispered, sniffing. Wally couldn't see even a trace of a cloud anywhere.

Granddad's hand moved from Wally's shoulder, and the old man cupped both palms to his mouth, leant back in supplication, and wailed 'Send her down, Hughie!' to the precipitation gathering over the plains to the southwest.

'Send her down, Hughie!' Wally added in a shrill echo of Granddad's prayer. Mickey looked up from the tree stump away to their left where he was licking blood off his paws, and put his ears back.

In the silence, Wally fancied he could see wisps of white in the haze.

Granddad patted him on the back, and they descended towards the homestead. Mickey ran ahead yipping all the way, which Mum heard, and told Alice to put the kettle on.

When Dad came in from the neighbour's, Granddad watched

from the verandah as Wally and Alice ran in the golden light into the arms of his son. There were three head on the tray, and the kids were heaved up to look at the new purchases. Three glowing rams. Granddad could see the quality, even from a distance.

Before he went in, he spied the tree, gently rocking in the breeze. To the southwest was indigo sky, and not a trace of cloud. He shook his head and retreated indoors. The kids were yelling by then, and his son wouldn't stop them.

THE bucket sloshed around Wally's legs. He was already running late, but every day since Granddad died, Dad made him carry a bucket of water up the hill behind the house and pour it on the tree. If he missed the school bus it was an hour's walk and explanation to the teacher and lines or sums and no play lunch.

This morning it was hot by breakfast. Wally had a corner of toast in his free hand, the sweet marmalade at the edges of his mouth as he panted his way up with his shoulder stretched by the weight of it. Alice didn't come up with him anymore. Not even Mickey did much.

The only respite would come if it had rained. Then Wally could sleep in for a week, until Dad started looking up at the sky every time he went outdoors and slid his hat on his head. But it hadn't rained for weeks now.

The tree rose from the knee-high grass. Now a foot taller than Wally, with a handmade well he'd refashioned last year from Granddad's original. The fir of the branches had filled out and pricked Wally's forearms as he sloshed the water around the base of the growing trunk, and the last of it over his scorched forehead to cool down.

Then, in real hope of reprieve from Granddad's daily sentence, Wally turned to the southwest as he always did and called to the sky: 'Send her down, Hughie!' sometimes muttering, 'please,' which was picked up by the dry wind and evaporated before it even carried a few metres.

On this day, the shrill edge of Wally's voice was not there. Wally screeched then growled, swallowing the prayer and trying again. This time, a man's voice bellowed down the hillside and flew off in the direction of the town. Wally felt it go, the tingling of it all the way to his toes, pressing against the inside of his shoes.

A few minutes and a short sprint later, he tossed the bucket under the water tank with a metallic rattle and ran into the side door of the kitchen. Alice was standing on a stool at the sink washing up.

'Clear your things!' she cried as he passed through into the hall.

'Clear them yourself!' Wally boomed. He waited for an answer. Granddad would've walloped him. Dad was already gone, and the school bus was sending up dust only a mile from the faded sign which told the passerby the name of the farm, Willow Way.

Alice still had soap on her elbows as she just made the bus. Her brother was already up the back with the other boys.

'I know something that you don't,' she said to her brother in front of everyone.

'Yeah? What about?' Wally jeered, folding his arms.

'About your stupid buckets of *water*,' Alice said, thumping herself into the empty seat, ignoring the wall of jeers.

Mum watched the bus disappear from the kitchen window as she finished the dishes.

The water was dirty, but they'd need to use it until the end of the week. She strained the grease off the surface, and shooed the dogs off the doorstep.

NORTH of the town, a left turn at the crossroads, then another left turn at the patch of willow trees and up to the tablelands, an old sign sent you to the right up a crooked lane, then plunged you down again across a ford over a creek. The same creek which kept the willow trees alive about three miles downstream.

Up a little hill, past a derelict farmhouse, through a fallen gate, was Wally's own place.

Dad had agreed to help him buy it, but he refused to help him farm it.

'You'll get it up and running, just like we all did here at Willow Way,' Dad whined through gritted teeth the day Wally moved out of home, passing an arm across the land his father and grandfather had farmed years before him.

Wally looked away, got back to tying the last of the furniture on the back of his ute, and slid into the cabin.

As he turned the vehicle away from Dad, Mum waving up on the verandah, he spied Granddad's tree atop the hillside. He hadn't been pricked by that bloody tree for years now. It stood three times taller than him.

'Water it yourself,' he'd said to Dad one day, before hitching a ride into town to see a rerun of *King Kong* at the flicks at the big town to the south. There were always girls there, at least one to sit next to every boy.

Every week, Wally would do something more to his farm. First it was getting rid of the trees growing inside the bedrooms, or cutting back the blackberry that threatened to overtake the kitchen through the rotten floors.

He nicked supplies from the derelict house closer to the main road – weatherboards, iron roof sheeting, old light fixtures – and soon the place was sealed against the wind and the rain.

On this side of town, nothing shielded you from the sou'westers like the hill did at Willow Way. A weathered sign on the main road pointed you to Windy Hill Farm.

They got that right, Wally bravely told himself the first weekend he spent retrieving roofing sheets from the gully. He placed them back on the skeleton of hardwood that was his house, and screwed them in tight this time.

Dad and Mum came around to announce Alice was marrying a farmer's son from over the state border. March wedding. He was in pigs. Had his own slaughterhouse and a few trucks, this Gerald.

Dad was proud. Mum did her son's dishes and baked some scones with the last of the flour she could scrape together from the canisters.

'Get yourself a wife,' Dad said to him as they sucked beers on the verandah, 'and you can have the rest of the money your Granddad wanted you to have, buy yourself a harvester. Land's so flat up here you may as well have your own harvester, you can borrow a plough from Dougie Myles, Georgie's boy. You should always work with your neighbours.'

'Yeah?' Wally said, raising an eyebrow but not looking at his father, who'd kicked every part of the house he could get his feet near. So far he hadn't found any places where the boards came up, or the nails weren't holding.

Wally forgot about how much that annoyed him and thought about turning up at the saleyards with some guarantee behind him. He could try twenty Hereford cows and a bull, and some sorghum between the house and the gully where it was already flat.

Mum came in with the scones. There was no tea left. She'd heard the rats nesting underneath the fuel stove, could hear the young ones that would have been born after her son arrived. *Opportunists*, she always thought, of vermin. Mickey was long dead, the best ratter they ever had. The two white dogs on her son's verandah were too sound asleep to hear anything.

But she didn't say anything. She swept the kitchen floor and used her forearm to measure how wide she'd need to make the curtains she'd bring next time they came around. If there was going to be a wife here, she'd need something nice about the place to make her stay.

She watched Dad and Wally walking out to the shed. Wally was already waving his arms which meant Dad wasn't listening. She'd hear all about it on the way home.

As they ascended the hill after the creek, all Dad said was: 'Dry over this side. Stock'll only break up the topsoil.' He tutted, looked both ways, turned onto the bitumen and cast a glance across his son's land as he adjusted his hat.

'Send her down, Hughie,' he prayed, biting his lip and shaking his head. In a mile he spotted the pine tree on his own hill, and turned the truck to follow it home.

CAROLYN was from the coast. She spied Wally at the local Ball and picked him out from all the other ruddy-faced youths who lined the bar at least ten thick under the marquee, set up to save space inside the country hall for dancing. Her friend Phyllida was already dancing with some guy in a pale suit.

'He's nice,' Phyllida whispered into Carolyn's ear, pointing out how tall Wally was. Carolyn was a tall girl, and she needed a tall man to keep her in scale.

She stuck with some other girls until one by one they were all taken and danced with. Wally took his time. She nearly went with at least two others, both shorter, still looking for Wally in the crowd. It took him an hour to finally come over and ask her if she wanted a drink, then another half an hour for him to get her one from the bar, and another half for him to ask her to dance.

He dipped her hand like a plough as they parted the crowd. She laughed at him, trying to squeeze his hand and make him relax. He drew breath and laughed with his mouth open. She bit her lip. He was handsome up close, and she needed to lift her chin to look him in the eyes.

He telephoned her the next week, from the phone box at the shop in town. Her Dad boomed down the line at him, trying to ascertain who it was calling his only daughter. When Carolyn finally got on the line he didn't really know what to say.

'How's the weather there girl?' Wally blurted. She laughed. 'Dry out here,' he added, 'we need rain.' She agreed he could drive to the coast the next weekend and take her out to lunch.

He got his hair cut in town the day before, waited in the good room while Mum fixed his best shirt, and got out that bottle of aftershave his sister had given him for Christmas three years ago.

'Who's the lucky girl then?' people asked him. Most were pleased to see him making plans to land a wife, but some said there was nothing wrong with the local girls.

They were married after a false start. Carolyn was due to sail to Britain the year they met, and nearly cancelled, but her father made her go, thinking it would be enough to see her in the arms of someone else by the end of the year.

Mum reassured Wally, came around as much as she could, commented on the paintwork to the dry boards of the house, and the wallpaper job he did in the old hallway. The place was looking better, every time.

'Had a letter from Carolyn this week?' she always asked.

'Yeah,' Wally said, smoothing his hands over the latest letter as though that would tell him what Paris, or Berlin, or London was like.

At the end of every day he'd sit with the dogs on the verandah watching the last of the light on the backs of the cows in the field towards the main road, and plan what he'd do the next day, another day closer to her coming home.

Wally drove to Sydney to meet her off the boat. Slept in his car two nights on the way and spruced himself up in the dunny at the Woolloomooloo docks.

He borrowed a suit from Dad and looked quite the dandy in the welcoming crowds. Carolyn's Dad was there, so was Phyllida. She put an arm through Wally's and pulled him to her.

'You're going to make Carolyn very happy,' she said.

Carolyn's father shook his hand, trying to get an arm past the bunch of flowers Wally had found that morning.

When Carolyn spotted them all from the ship she looked between Dad and Wally. Phyllida pointed to Wally and mouthed, *what a charmer.*

At lunch, Wally refused to let her father pay. He'd sold some of the first calves and kept the best for next year.

When Phyllida went to powder her nose, and her father went to order another drink, Carolyn leant towards Wally and they kissed. A peck, then a lingering welcome home.

They married three months later at the coast. Wally's Mum and Dad stayed at the hotel on The Point and Dad couldn't stop raving about the quality of the place and the service and why hadn't they come years before?

Alice and Gerald came across the border with their two girls and a tray of pork so large the hotel had to clear out the fridges just to store it.

Dad raved about that too, and got drunker laughing at course after course of pork and bacon coming out of the kitchen. Mum kicked him under the table but he slurred: 'Don't you worry old girl,' which made her look down, in her lemon-coloured hat and gloves, and wish herself away.

After the Gold Coast honeymoon, Wally drove Carolyn home the inland way. They dropped in on Mum and Dad for a scone and a cuppa and to collect the dogs.

Willow Way put on a good show, a solid old homestead at the end of a long drive with whitewashed stones every few metres. The home yard was full of deep green grass.

Wally finally saw his mother in a new light, perched on her chair holding out trays of tarts and making sure Carolyn had all she wanted.

Mum had tried to insist he bring Carolyn around tomorrow. She'd been out to Windy Hill Farm for a night, getting the place ready for the honeymooners' return, and muttered something about Willow Way being an embarrassment of riches compared to Wally's place.

But Wally had insisted: 'It's on our way Mum, don't fuss.'

Wally was drunk on lovemaking, on having his way with a woman, and Carolyn had given herself to him, absolutely, so he wasn't going to hear anything untoward from Mum or Dad.

The dogs barked their delight at seeing him, and he mastered them for Carolyn by barking orders back until they were up on the tray, ready to go home.

The drive took only twenty minutes, through the shreds of the town, past the closed shops and the derelict church, then up to the tablelands and across the creek.

The truck wobbled its way across the current and the boulders, and the dogs got the scent of their land and started yipping with delight, making Carolyn laugh.

'Never fails, this creek,' Wally announced proudly.

'Really?' Carolyn answered, turning to spy the abundant reeds and the white lilies flowering in the shade. She thought he would stop, but he wanted to crest the hill and hoped the cattle were grazing at this end of the yard in front of the homestead, so that it all looked perfect.

There was one cow at this end. The rest were in the shade of a half-fallen tree. Dad had piled up the feed there.

'Here we are,' Wally announced, spreading an arm in his best impersonation of Granddad.

'Lovely,' she said, skipping inside before he could carry her over the threshold. One of the dogs saw the rat scuttle across the kitchen floor, but missed it after rushing past her.

'Get out of it!' Wally yelled.

'Not to worry,' Carolyn said, holding out her hand to receive his.

'They'll listen to you, soon enough,' he said.

'Plenty of time,' she hushed him, 'bring my bags?'

She noticed every little touch of him in the house. Every little attempt at nicety that she could finish off. This was all she wanted, a place she could make her own, away from the coast, the endless terrace parties and 'do's' at the club.

The home yard wasn't green yet, but the creek held a moist promise that Carolyn already had her eye on.

WALLY planted sorghum in the naked field between the house and the gully. It was easy work. Had it done in a few hours. The machinery ripped open the earth with such a lightness that he was distracted from the dust that showed the topsoil was drifting away, swept over the flat land towards the fold of the creek, and caught by the damp air there, feeding the reeds and the willows.

Mum took Carolyn to Ladies' Cards and made her a stack of friends amongst the neighbouring farmers' wives.

Margie Myles was the friendliest. She had a row of blonde kids already and knew Carolyn would be needing to furnish a nursery soon enough, so she promised to set aside all the baby essentials any new bride would need.

Carolyn was two months gone when the sorghum shoots showed

themselves through the remaining soil.

'All we need's a good drop of rain, and they'll raise themselves,' Wally said, splashing the nice drinks she'd prepared on the verandah, and getting dirt where she'd swept twice that day. He downed a cold beer and held his glass out for another, then leapt off the verandah onto the patch of grass seed she'd sewn, bent his back, tilted his neck up and shouted: 'Send her down, Hughie!'

Carolyn cocked her head and giggled: 'What's that mean?'

'Never mind love,' was all he could think to say.

'SOMETHING for the grandkids,' Dad said, trying to convince Wally that the right thing to do was to sell Willow Way and move into town.

Wally sighed a couple of times, trying to get his head around the idea, half expecting Granddad to clip him around the ear.

Dad was sitting in his office, with the view stretching down the drive towards the town. Mum and Carolyn were playing with the kids in the front room.

Outside it was bucketing down. Sheets of rain had been slapping the iron roofing of homes across the district for days. Creeks were up. There was no way out of town to the south or the west, 'unless you had a boat,' Georgie Myles had announced at the RSL Club the night before.

Georgie Myles had his eye on Willow Way for his son and his young family. Georgie was of farming stock himself, but further west where the hills were kinder to flocks of sheep, and he'd sold up a decade ago and been enjoying the high life in a big new house on the edge of town where Martha, his wife, kept an acre of garden and an acre of orchard, just to keep her hand in.

Mum and Dad had been spending more time there so that they didn't have to drive back after Mum's visits to the hospital. They wouldn't say what it was, only: 'You're not to worry.'

Wally knew they'd told Alice but no one was telling him.

'Your Granddad made provision for you and Alice, and left me out of it,' Dad said. 'He was a rich old bugger by the time he died, and you've had the benefit of all that, you and Alice, so Mum and I have decided we'll do the same for your three and Alice's two. When they reach their twenty-first birthdays it'll be theirs, whatever we don't need to live on.'

Wally couldn't take it all in. He was pleased for his three boys, the new one only a month old, but not having this place to visit? He couldn't see why Dad was giving it up. Dad stood up from his desk and pointed to the framed map on the wall. The familiar contours of the hill and the river, which ran dry so often the blue line encircled the eastern half of the property like a lie.

'We'll sell here, and here,' Dad said, pointing to the left where he'd made arrangements already. 'Billy Bryant's wanted that lot since we were at school, and that'll give me and Mum a chance to build a place in town. Then when that's done Georgie's promised me a good price for the rest.'

Wally heard it but he was looking at the map. There was Willow Way, a little black square by the hill, but over by the river were other little black squares. 'What's there?' Wally pointed.

'The old farm,' Dad said, not looking, 'long gone. Built it in the wrong spot, or some such nonsense. Now I've written to Alice and

Gerald and there's to be no squabbles or we'll give it all to the dogs' home, alright?'

'Alright,' Wally said, watching his father stretch his arms out for a grandson on each side in the hallway.

LATER that spring, the rains eased and the sorghum lifted higher than it had ever been at Windy Hill Farm. Carolyn took a photo of all the boys on Dad's bike, the crop behind them so abundant that she was filled with a sense of hope.

By November, the rains were gone and so was all the moisture from the soil. The sorghum withered. They'd been trying pigs but the pigs got out and finished off the sorghum overnight. They had enough money after selling off the pigs to plan for another crop or more stock.

When she saw the money go into Wally's back pocket as he headed back towards the car after the sale, Carolyn started dandling the baby and decided she'd persuade Wally to try something different this time. Between the saleyards and home she'd make him see.

Wally was temporarily mollified by the money and had his mind on a trip to the pub that evening when the kids were in bed.

She'd been on at him to make an office in one of the rooms off the verandah, 'just like your father's', so when she started with that tone as they passed through the town, he was already defensive.

'The crops have never worked on the gully side. Why don't we try them on the creek side?'

'I've already told you,' he wailed, 'we can't afford the equipment to cultivate it.'

'We could borrow a plough from Dougie and Margie, we've got the harvester already.'

'I'm not going borrowing from him.'

'Can't we just try it, one season?' she pleaded, looking away as he made the turn up to the tablelands. The land slid past them, replete with burgeoning crops on either side, down where it was flat and the water table high, and there were windbreaks from the killer sou-westerlies.

'Listen love, I don't tell you what's best for the boys or the house, do I?'

She was silent, wanting to say it would be a nice change if he did.

As they turned off the main road the swollen creek greeted them. Over the last year negotiating it in the old ute was getting harder because it was deeper and wider. The willows had made their way upstream and now drank the abundant water from both sides, and bullrushes and lilies grew up the muddy banks towards their front field. Some of the sorghum blown from the gully had taken in the shelter between the fence and the creek and was ready for harvesting.

Wally went away for a weekend to a seed conference. Carolyn said she was going to do some renovating while he was gone. He nodded, kissed her, and left.

Before the dust from his disappearing ute had settled, she'd opened the gate, whistled up the dogs and had the cows on their way to the gully field where there was still feed from the failed crop.

She called Dougie Myles and had him plough and sew the front field by sundown. Dougie asked no questions and Carolyn just plied him with sandwiches and barley water until it was done.

'Have any problems with the soil?' she asked.

'Nope. Good as gold. Bit woody near the creek, but the water table's high up that end. Good and high. Best place to plant, worse place for stock. Anyhow, I'll be off.'

'Let me pay you.'

'Nah, just send Wally around with the harvester when he's done this lot. I'll plant in a week so we'll be ready a week after you.'

'Thanks Dougie, say hi to Margie,' she said.

Dougie headed for his new dual-cab ute, and she noticed the baby seat strapped into the back. Wally never let her buy one. *Just hold them in the front* was his way.

There were clouds in the south, gathering over the foothills near the town. The child on her hip seemed to notice them too, and gave a little gurgle. Dougie waved as Carolyn arched her back, cupped her spare hand to her mouth and tilted her head back.

'Send her down, Hughie!' she called.

Dougie heard it from the creek as he crossed, thinking it was a crow calling others to the freshly ploughed field.

He shivered at the silence after the call, although by the time he was back at the main road, he'd forgotten all about it.

WALLY refused to harvest the crop, but watched Dougie Myles bring in the sorghum in their front field with Wally's harvester in about two hours. They sold it the next day.

Carolyn didn't lord anything over him. She just asked for half the money and went into town to buy new shoes for the older boys, a new frock for herself, and, with a hopeful air, a beautiful skein of wool to knit Wally a jumper. Autumn would soon be closing in. They'd been lucky to get that last crop in.

Something about the way she left for town made him head west to meet Fiona at the club. She was a smart blonde. Older than him but still pretty, the freckly country kind of pretty, and she wore jodhpurs. All the men in the club could see her fine arse and Wally liked that. They kissed in the cabin of his ute and rekindled the night of passion at the seed conference by doing it in the truck behind the service station.

He told Carolyn he'd been at the pub.

Two weeks later their boys found the youngest, the baby, dead in his cot. Wally tried to give his son mouth-to-mouth, struggling to recall first aid classes from thirty years ago at the town pool, but the cold lips of the baby gave no response.

They lay the dead child in its bassinet between the other boys and drove into Mum and Dad's, left the boys there, and took the body to the hospital.

CAROLYN sat in the box at the side of the court house, her eyes glazed over. The magistrate cleared his throat, shuffled through the papers in front of him, and thanked the psychologist, who stepped down from the witness box and walked back to the public gallery.

Wally was up there, eyes on the floor. Two of his mates from school were a few rows back, but he wished they would leave. His parents sat away to the side. Mum was purse-lipped and decked out like it was church. Dad hid his shock under a broad hat.

A young policeman read out the charge list, recounting the day they'd called at Windy Hill Farm after the new shopping centre had apprehended Carolyn shoplifting for the second time.

Mum shifted in her seat. She'd always offered to make the boys' clothes. She looked at her daughter-in-law, slumped like a lazy willow, and couldn't take any of it in.

The magistrate cleared his throat, which woke them all from their stupor, and duly asked the defendant to stand.

He told Carolyn the seriousness of her crimes and the due punishment that would be meted out to her, how many days in the women's prison, a day's drive away, was warranted for each item of children's clothing she had stolen.

Carolyn heard every word, reminded of her father's admonishing tone when she and her cousins had scared a young child off a bike, and felt the acid burning inside over something so wrong, and that she'd been the cause. She was already too far from the musty safeness of her children's embraces, and now she was slipping further away.

'In the light of the psychological report, and the recent loss of a child in sudden circumstances,' the magistrate said, looking up to the assembled crowd, 'the court will suspend the sentence pending a good behaviour bond and an assurance of continued psychiatric treatment.'

'Agreed,' Carolyn's lawyer said, half standing.

'That satisfies me,' the magistrate said. Carolyn didn't move immediately, so the magistrate muttered to the attendant at the side: 'Send her down.'

DOUGIE Myles had two sons, one of whom farmed Willow Way when Dougie and Margie took up prawn farming on the coast.

Stevie Myles and his wife Sharon repainted the old homestead a bright blue everyone reckoned you could almost see from the town.

Sharon was a successful dog breeder and Stevie built her a row of kennels where the old sheep yards had been.

Before Stevie left school he'd read on the internet about growing olive trees, and in the eroded gullies of the hillside he planted groves of them. For the first year he carted the water up the hill by hand, then installed a hose pipe and eventually a series of tanks.

The year the abattoir closed, an Asian corporation announced they were building an olive oil refinery at the crossroads of the old town. You could see it going up from the north-facing hillside where Stevie tended his trees. He had a herd of goats free-ranging, keeping the blackberry out of the gullies and the weeds off the hillside.

One afternoon, two blokes drove up the drive in a low city car. They got out and one of them introduced himself. Mark, his name was, said he was the great grandson of the family who built the old house by the creek.

'Not there anymore mate,' Stevie said, 'too damp along there for a house, they reckon. D'you know the old tree up on the hill? The old man carried water up there every day.'

Mark nodded. He looked as though he knew the story, but didn't really want to hear it again.

'Do ya wanna look around?' Stevie asked. The two blokes looked at one another. One shrugged, the other nodded. 'Where you live then?' Stevie asked.

'The city,' Mark said.

'Hey Sharon love, this is Wally Taylor's boy ... remember? From Windy Hill Farm.'

A woman in a denim skirt had emerged onto the verandah, two little dogs at her feet and one on her hip.

'Yeah?' she squinted. 'Your family's been gone from round here for ages, ay?'

'Yes,' Mark said.

'Well, do you want to come in for a cuppa tea?' Sharon asked.

'Gonna show them around first love,' Stevie said.

Mark was tapping his foot against the car, looking as though he would have liked a cup of tea.

'You the older brother?' Sharon said to the other bloke, licking the dust from the road off her teeth.

'No, this is Peter,' Mark said. 'My partner,' he added.

'Right,' Stevie said, flicking the flies off his shoulders, and letting out a little laugh.

'Welcome back then,' Sharon added, throwing a stern look that released her husband from his frozen spot, the same way she did when he got all stupid about the gays at the dog shows.

'Yeah, welcome back,' Stevie said.

'It's a beaut piece of land this,' Sharon said, compensating for her husband. 'Your family chose it well when they got it. Gees, must've been over a hundred years ago I reckon.'

'Yeah, a hundred years, eh?' Stevie added.

'We were sorry to hear about your Mum,' Sharon piped up, and added, with courage, 'terrible thing, cancer.'

Mark nodded, looking as though he was grateful of the mention.

'Your Dad come across for the funeral?' she asked.

'Nope,' Mark said.

'He's a seed supplier now, didn't we hear that love?' Stevie asked.

'Yeah, we got a catalogue last winter, remember?' she said.

'Oh yeah,' Stevie remembered.

'Had this bit written about him, on the back cover, like his life story or something,' Sharon laughed. 'The way he put it, he might never have even had kids or a wife or anything. Kinda odd, we thought.'

'Yeah,' Stevie added, 'like his life started when he took up with that other sheila.'

A silence. They all nodded.

'Well, see you back here in a bit,' Sharon waved them off.

Stevie showed them across to the machine shed where his ute was already facing up the hill.

'Wanna put that on the back?' he asked, indicating the blue bag Mark clutched at his side.

'It's okay,' Mark replied, holding it closer.

Stevie shrugged, whistled for his dogs, and they jumped on the tray. He pulled a tarpaulin out of the footwell, which sent straw and dust out over the two other men.

When they immediately dusted themselves off, Stevie said: 'Gees, sorry!' and laughed. 'Let's see the tree then, or what's left of it.'

The three of them squeezed into the ute and swayed in unison as the terrain got rough.

'You're alright,' Stevie said to Pete, who was so large he had to hold his leg away from bouncing off Stevie's hand on the gear stick.

The sun was harsher up the hill. Peter took a photo of Mark standing by the tree stump, looking as though he wanted to get back in the ute and drive back down to his own car.

'I don't remember it at all,' Mark said. 'I was only told of it, and I have a photo of my great grandfather standing in front of it with my Dad.'

'Yeah?' Stevie said, thinking he must get the dogs up here more often to cull a few rabbits.

'What's down there?' Peter asked, pointing to the deep shade at the bend of the river.

'That's our willow tree tangle,' Stevie said. 'Only willows left on the place now, I reckon.'

They piled back into the ute, dropped down the hill and headed for the river. Where the scrubby yellow straw ended, bright green garden grass had taken over, and Stevie pulled up.

'Can't drive any further, we'll never get out of there if I do,' he said, thinking he should get the grader over and knock a few of the willows down to dry the place up a bit.

MARK stepped out of the ute before it came to a stop, the blue bag tucked under one arm.

He'd already spied where the ancient willow trunks had fallen and dammed the pools, many years ago. The new season's leaves were starting to block the modest path of the water.

This was something he did remember.

'Water table's rising,' he whispered.

All those times his Dad and Grandfather had taken his older brother up the hill, he'd hidden under the old water tank where no one came looking, and crept back into Nanna's kitchen.

She'd given him little errands to run, checking she'd found every egg in the chook yard, or picked her bits of this and that from the kitchen garden.

One afternoon, they'd walked beyond the home yard with the retired working dogs.

Mum was there, and Aunty Alice and the cousins, and Nanna told them the story of the old house that once stood where the willow trees grew.

She showed them the remnants of the original soil slab, and the well, full of rocks now where her old mother-in-law had filled it in so her children couldn't fall in after they got the town water.

'Your Grandfather carted water up that hill every day until it killed him,' she'd told the children, watching the men up on the hill, shaking her head, 'but all you have to do is look for the water table,' she added.

'Never look for water up high, you'll always have to cart it up high, but down low, you'll always find moisture.'

Mark drew breath when he saw the rows of purple irises either side of where the old pathway led up to the house long gone.

He and Mum had picked them that day. Now they'd spread further than the path, in an unbridled swathe between willow trunks all the way to the water.

He pulled the plastic box from the blue bag and walked through the lilies.

'What's he got there?' Stevie asked Peter.

'His mum's ashes,' Peter whispered.

Stevie stopped, leaned on the bonnet, and muttered: 'Righty-o.'

'We couldn't get onto the land at Windy Hill Farm,' Peter explained, 'and there's none of her family left at the coast. Mark just wanted somewhere to put them, you know, before we go back tomorrow.'

Stevie nodded, mouth pulled into a knot. He wasn't about to say anything, but it just fell out of him. 'Good place for her, I reckon,' he said. The two men stopped and look back at him, so it was right that he explain. 'My Mum used to say yours must've got it into her head about planting that sorghum crop near the creek from somewhere.'

Mark's face reddened with emotion. 'What crop?'

'The only complete crop your Dad ever got off Windy Hill Farm,' Stevie replied. 'Your Mum was known for it around here, until, well ... you know,' and closed his mouth with a snap.

In the silence, the tiniest of rapids sounded from the river bend.

'Where does this water go?' Mark asked.

Stevie sniffed, and said: 'South for a ways, then it joins the big river. Runs all the way to the coast and empties into the sea.'

Mark nodded. *This is the right place*, but he started to struggle with the lid of the plastic box.

Peter didn't hesitate. He went to Mark's side and deftly pulled the tape off. Inside was another plastic bag with a small tie they both pulled at until it came away.

As he pressed his hand into the ashes, they reminded Mark momentarily of the wood of the stricken tree stump.

The three men watched the first grey cloud settle onto the surface of the dark water and ease its way towards the ripple that gave onto to the rapids.

'*Send her down*,' Mark whispered, the dust on his cheek giving way to his tears.

Closet His Closet Hers

His

THEIR MENTOR RODNEY had been telling them about homosexuals and how they can get around God's will for you. Something about the smallness of the room, and the closeness between all the young men, made Wayne's penis hard, especially when Rodney clapped him on the back.

He waited until the others had gone, touched his toes, and laughed when Bruce said: 'What's up with you?'

'Just stretching,' Wayne replied, 'leg's gone to sleep,' he lied, rubbing his calf like the way the coach did at footy.

Bruce jeered and disappeared for hot chocolates with the rest. The girls' group had finished first and already there were raised voices. Someone was singing a hymn in a jazz style, and some of the boys were joining in.

Wayne didn't dare leave the room until he was quite soft in his shorts.

Later that night, he lay awake, his sleeping bag too hot in the warm room which smelled of feet. Bruce snored in the bunk above him, turning in his sleep and muttering comfortable noises into the silence.

Wayne knew Bruce had red undies on, he'd spied the edges showing through the dark crevice either side of his shorts. Bruce always had his long legs pulled up out of everyone's way, so it was easy enough to get a glimpse. Was Wayne the only one who noticed how much pubic hair you could see?

It was just something he noticed. That's all.

He sighed, turned onto his back, and jerked off thinking of Annabelle from school, her surprised face becoming even more animated as he imagined her watching him. Perhaps she'd run her hands along the back of his legs?

But towards the end she turned into Bruce, those long legs with those red pants around his ankles, nestled in the black satiny football shorts, while Wayne tugged at him.

He exploded and was out cold in minutes. Tomorrow he'd ask God for help again.

'EVERYTHING alright, mate?' Rodney asked, not looking up from buttering slices of breakfast toast.

'Yeah, aw yeah,' Wayne drawled.

'Something come up from one of the sessions mate?' Rodney asked, unwrapping another loaf, snapping the plastic away into the bin in a sporty motion.

'I think so,' Wayne said, voice brittle.

Rodney put the knife up between them, a knob of cheap margarine on its end. 'We'll sort it out mate, that's what we're here for, okay? God can sort anything out, if only we ask.'

Rodney clapped him on the back again, then disappeared, yelling for two volunteers from the shouting basketball crowd to set the table.

RODNEY and another mentor called Bill were sitting in the common room, leaning forward with their elbows on their knees.

Bill spied Wayne first, and smiled.

'G'day mate,' Bill said, 'I'm gonna sit in and help Rodney with this session, if that's okay?'

'Just church policy,' Rodney said, 'but you can say whatever you want to both of us, okay?'

Just then two girls came through asking permission to change the video in the other common room. The boys and girls had been put in together because of Wayne's special meeting, although the girls didn't know that before. They did now. One of them, Sharon, cocked an eyebrow at Wayne.

'Bugger off you two,' Rodney said, 'you can watch one after the other. Boys' video first.'

'Don't worry mate,' Bill said, 'that's what this camp's for, sorting out issues for you kids. Video time's just one issue. Quiet time with us is another, so what's on your mind?'

Wayne looked at the floor. Somewhere that day he'd scuffed his new track shoes. There were black streaks down the inside edge of both of them, like he'd been nervously scraping them on something.

'Would you like to pray?' Rodney asked after a minute. Wayne nodded. 'Holy Father, be with us now while Wayne struggles to ask you in. Clear the air for us to help him and open his heart to whatever's on his mind.'

Wayne hardly heard it. The other men had their heads down. His was too, but then he looked up.

Bill was tanned. His short-sleeved shirt was striped blue and white, and his heavy forearms were laced with thick black hairs. There was only half a metre between Wayne and those arms. He could reach out and hold them, and the distance would be covered in a second.

'God's big enough,' Rodney said, lifting his head. Wayne flicked his eyes down.

'Girls, is it?' Bill asked, but not like a question, like he'd decided he already knew. 'It happens, young fella, and at a different age for everyone. It's like you don't know what to say, and your body's doing all sorts of strange things, and you think you're the only one, am I right Rodney?'

'Oh yeah. Been through that one, but we all live to tell the tale. God's there though, as long as you stay open to him. Are you open to him Wayne?'

Wayne looked between the two pairs of eyes. He nodded and looked down at his shoes again.

'Right then,' Rodney said, standing and clapping Wayne on the back. 'I better go save video night from disaster.'

Bill nodded, but indicated he'd stay a moment. Wayne could feel him looking, and didn't want to look up because he was afraid of what he'd see.

'Sometimes things come we don't want, things that scare us. Perhaps you're having things like that?'

In the other room Rodney was yelling orders for kids to sit down and put on the video.

Wayne shrugged. It was enough. Bill adjusted his frame in the chair and thrust his hands forward.

'Don't you worry about that mate, God's big enough for that too. You just need to ask him for special help, to put you back onto the right track, you–'

Rodney was at the door, Bill's eyes flicked away and he leant back in his chair.

'I think we need to bring the boys in here,' Rodney decided out loud.

'Righto,' Bill said, lower than before. He stood, clapped Wayne on the back, his shorts brushing the younger man's shoulder as he passed.

Wayne stayed until the other boys came in, so he scored the best seat for the video.

They watched *Top Gun*. It was a copied tape so there were edits in the sex scene, at which they all roared, making Rodney shout, 'when you're older!' over the mock complaints.

Later, at hot chocolates, Bill was busy. Two girls were helping, and he noticed Wayne watching him when he turned from the sink at the far end of the kitchenette. The older man smiled.

THE next year, Wayne did all he could to end his friendship with Bruce. He gave up footy training and shrugged whenever Mum said 'ask Bruce around if you like.'

Winter Bible Camp was postponed when Bill Timmins was sacked from the school he'd worked at for fifteen years.

'Turns out he was one of those *homosexuals*,' Mum said to Mrs Callaghan on the phone. 'I don't know how I'm going to tell Wayne's father,' she added, lowering her voice.

Wayne chucked in swimming club the week the freestyle captain, John Bate, who was a year ahead of Wayne, made everyone show their pubes in the change shed and accused one kid of 'getting a stiffy'.

John was a big guy with a lot of hair between his legs. He entered

Wayne's fantasies and stayed longer than anyone had ever before. Wayne imagined John forcing him into showing all sorts of things, but from a distance, from across the change room, sometimes standing up on the change benches the way they all did so they didn't get warts on their feet.

Bible Camp came around again, and Mum made him go because there was no alternative. She and Dad were going to a wedding in Queensland. 'You'll just be bored,' she said, filling out the booking forms. She packed his clean clothes the way she always did, sighing when it was all done, as though two weeks away from dirty laundry was going to be nice.

There was talk on the bus about Mr Timmins. Some said he'd tried to kiss a boy at school, but Brittany Melville said that was all nonsense.

'The school sacked him because it turned out he'd been living with another man,' she assured them at the back of the bus, away from the younger kids. 'A man he said was a flatmate from teachers' college, but one of the school mothers had a brother who was a plumber who did some work at the house and found out there was only one bedroom with a double bed in it, and a statue of a naked man in the back garden.'

Rodney noticed the secretive energy, and told them all to face the front.

When they arrived at the little huts nestled in the bush by the river, Bruce and Todd decided they'd share a room this year. Wayne was left with Shawn, a younger kid who sniffled the whole way.

'Wayne'll look after you, won't you Wayne?' Rodney said as they gathered the kids' luggage from the bus. Wayne nodded unhappily, watching Bruce and the other boy racing to the end rooms.

There were more boys than girls that summer, so some of the boys had to have what were considered 'girl rooms' which were at one end of the girls' corridor, separated by an ill-fitting office divider.

That's where Wayne and Shawn ended up, since all the other rooms were taken while Wayne dragged the kid and his stupid bags up to the main door. As they inspected their digs, girls were looking through the cracks between the divider and the wall.

'Kissy-kissy,' one of them said, pouting wet lips.

Shawn must have farted because their room stank when Wayne pushed the door shut with a slam, making the kid jump in fright.

'I'll take the top bunk. I bet you still wet the bed,' Wayne blurted, flinging his bag up and marching out to lunch.

Bruce and Todd were watching for him when Wayne walked in. Most of the sandwiches were already gone, only a few stacks of the less popular fillings stood like fallen towers, piles of lettuce at their feet.

Others were on the terrace chasing birds off the handrails. Bruce sneered, and in a low voice said: 'How's your little poofter roommate?' Todd laughed, like it was his idea, and simply added: 'Yeah?'

Wayne found a chicken sandwich, scooped it up, and shoved it into his mouth. 'Fuck off Bruce,' he said, chewing.

'*Fuck off Bruce*,' Todd mimicked in a high-pitched voice, then laughed. 'Let's leave the bum chums to it,' he added, as Wayne felt the presence of Shawn at his shoulder, fishing out an egg sandwich for himself.

The other boys left and all Wayne could smell was egg, as Shawn chewed it so loudly the sound drowned everything else out.

There were no groups organised that day. The campers were left to swimming with a mentor supervising. Bruce and the other older boys took control of the tyre swing which they used to jump into the deep pool. Wayne could hear them shouting from the basketball courts up the hill. He'd come up here when Shawn wasn't looking. Getting away from the yelling and splashing gave him time to think.

He knew from experience that 'loner behaviour' was not tolerated at camp, and before long someone would notice he was absent and one of the staff would come looking for him. He didn't count on Shawn seeking him out first, but luckily he noticed the pale yellow T-shirt skirt around the water tanks before it noticed him, and he ducked into the toilets.

In the dank shade the echo of the boys was weirdly louder. Dry cicada shells and leaves lined the brown tiled floor of what was known as the 'top toilet block' and no one had cleaned it out since last summer. Through the high windows he watched Shawn scuff his way further up the hill, dawdle by the first of the staff huts, and then disappear into the scrub. They'd be after him pronto if he ended up getting all the way to the lookout.

Relieved, Wayne swung on one of the cubicle doors. The creaking sound was so loud he didn't hear the girls coming from the other way.

'Yuuuuck!' one of them said, 'stinks in here.'

Wayne swung the door closed and locked it.

'Anyone in here?' another one of them asked. He stayed silent. One of them sniffed.

'Did you see what Bruce Sanders was wearing? Ball grabbers!'

'Shhhhhh,' the first one said, 'there's someone in here.'

Wayne could smell their fags, and heard one of them stubbing hers, the sizzle of the ash going out.

'Who the fuck's in here?'

'It's no one Janelle. Paranoid,' then thongs scuffing and doors being pushed.

'Who is it?' Janelle demanded. Wayne could see her pink sandals underneath the door. 'I bet it's a boy,' she whispered.

'This is the girls', didn't you hear?' one of them shouted. 'Who's in there?'

One of them got down on her hands and knees, a fag smoking between her fingers, which she popped into her mouth as she peered under. Annabelle Taylor. She was shocked for a moment, then smiled at him. He couldn't think what else to do but smile back. She looked him in the eye and said, 'it's only poofy Shawn!'

'Yuck,' Janelle shouted.

'Go and tell a teacher,' Annabelle said. The other two scuffed their way out and back down the hill.

'Come out,' Annabelle said, 'before they get back.' Wayne silently did what he was told. She leant against the wall by the door, one foot up behind her bum, the fag smouldering at her thigh. She flicked her head indicating for him to go.

He had both hands in his pockets, and went to edge past her, when she giggled, drew his face to hers, pressed her lips to his, moved her head side to side the way she'd seen them do in the movies. He froze, hands still in his pockets, as she separated them.

'Wanna fag?' she offered. He nodded, put the dwindling stub to his lips and puffed. It made him cough, which he turned into a laugh and said: 'Thanks Annabelle.'

'You go back first, okay?' she assured.

'Okay then.'

'See you later Wayne,' she added, winking.

He ran back to his room intending to dig out his ball grabbers and push Bruce off the tyre.

LIGHTS out, and the sharp eyes of Joanne, the girls' counsellor, meant they never had another moment alone, but there was plenty of suggestive staring. A planned disco in another girl's room, at midnight on their last night, was found out because one of the younger girls dobbed.

There was the usual all-male session in the common room about sex and girls. Rodney held some of the older boys back at the end of it, including Wayne, Bruce and Todd, and talked about 'situations you can find yourself in which God might not think is the best for you.'

Todd didn't take it seriously, which made Terry focus on him more than anyone. 'Laugh if you like, but these things can happen. You can be in over your head before you know it, with a girl or maybe, you know, you've let yourself succumb to someone who doesn't have the best of intentions for you ...'

'Like what do you mean, Rodney?' Todd said, looking to see how Bruce would react. Bruce looked down, going red in the face.

'You want me to explain?' Rodney asked. 'You seriously want me to, or are you just a little bit too much of a joker Todd? I'm talking seriously about keeping you all on the path Jesus Christ intends for you. Think about it. Once you let all that in, you might not find your way back to the right path.'

They were all silent. They all knew what he was talking about.

Wayne knew then that Annabelle had saved him. It was all going to be alright. He hadn't really thought much about wanting to see Todd and Bruce changing in their room, not since she'd pashed him, and there was the promise of more.

IN the back of the bus on the way to the sports carnival, they sat together. 'When we get there, meet me up behind the old tuck shop, okay?' Annabelle whispered.

Wayne had to get out of the relay by pretending to have a groin injury, the kind the teachers didn't really want to know about because they didn't want to know about down there, and found her smoking by the rubbish skips.

She threw the fag away and enveloped him in her arms, moaning and licking, then gave him a shock by running both hands down his buttocks. He flinched like a horse, sniggering. It made him hard, and the relief flooded through his whole body for days. Saved.

Masturbating to images of running his own hands down the school Chaplain's bum didn't count. He only did stuff like that when he was really tired, and he remembered Rodney saying: 'Go easy on yourself, give God time.'

SCHOOL was finishing. Wayne's last year, and there was the scent of last chances in the air. He'd decided on Engineering at uni if he could get enough marks in the exams. Word was that Bruce had actually done it with Claire at the leadership camp. Todd had been expelled for stealing from lockers. Janelle had become a high achiever and Annabelle's mother made sure her daughter hung out with the smart set. Wayne had grown taller than all the other boys. They left him alone once he and Annabelle started holding hands walking between classes.

Annabelle wasn't allowed to go to leadership camp. Wayne ended up sharing with Rodney because they had odd numbers of students.

Rodney was a fastidious roommate, up before Wayne woke and he came to bed long after lights out. Wayne was always waiting to watch as the older man slipped out of his undies and into his pyjamas. Once, he must have dropped his pyjama pants in the dark, but there was light enough to see a completely naked man lean over to retrieve them. Wayne squeezed his eyes shut but the image wouldn't go.

At the formal, Wayne pressed Annabelle up against the wall in the wings of the auditorium so she could feel him. She laughed, almost surprised. 'What's brought this on?' she whispered from the folds of her blue lace dress. He didn't have an answer, only wanted her to make him feel that way again. She laughed as he ran his hands over her back, breathing onto her neck, but when he aimed a hand between her knees she stopped him and stepped away.

'No,' she said, then laughed 'no, no, no,' keeping it light. His hair was in disarray and his mouth wet with desperation. 'Not until we're married,' she asserted, smoothing her dress down, and smiling at him.

They kissed goodbye when he dropped her home in his mother's car. She patted him on the leg as she slipped out. 'Good luck in the exams,' she said, and was gone.

AT uni, Wayne saw the graffiti in the cubicles and knew what Rodney had been talking about all those years. He read the looks from the boys who hung around the union toilets, and almost fell when a tall European man puckered his lips and nodded his head towards a cubicle while Wayne was washing his hands. It made him hard, but he resisted.

He found his way into the sex shops in the city on the way to meeting others from his college at the movies. At first he never bought anything, just looked at the magazine covers and avoided eye contact with the Asian women at the counter, sure they were sniggering when he loitered at the section with naked men.

There were group shots. Men posing, jaws dropped in pleasure, but none were touching, or if they were there was a black dot over the point of contact.

He'd always arrive at the box office flush with excitement, acutely aware of smells, aftershave, sweat, and in love with at least one of his mates meeting for a flick.

Uni sports was out of bounds after he'd gotten an erection in the shower room. He'd never been surrounded by so much hairy naked male flesh.

So he stuck to laps in the pool, where he could silently watch while breaststroking behind some good looking swimmer who had no idea what a view Wayne was getting between his legs.

One weekend when a couple of college mates agreed to meet at a different cinema, Wayne got lost on the way and ducked into a sex shop he'd not seen before. There were booths with coin slots.

There on the screen he saw the insertion, the sucking, the deep exchange between two men.

A knock on the door awoke him. 'Coins gentlemen!' came the demand. He'd been staring into space. As he fumbled for a coin he saw eyes staring at him through a hole in the wall.

They disappeared, and a fully erect penis was inserted through the hole. It swung in the semi darkness, and the sound of a coin falling was followed by porn music and male panting.

He looked at the penis, heard someone clear their throat, and moan, 'go on.'

He was out the door, down the stairs and purchasing his ticket to the movie before he could fall any further.

THERE was a school reunion only a year after they'd left. Someone suggested they go out to camp. No mentors or teachers. Janelle organised it and Wayne heard Annabelle was going. She was at another uni doing Arts or something.

Everyone arrived in separate cars, distant yet familiar, talking uni and jobs and how each was doing, who was too much of a snob to come to the reunion. Janelle was married and she and her husband Tim allocated rooms to everyone. No one shared. There were plenty of rooms to go around.

A great cry went up when Bruce arrived with his wife, a really pretty girl from Brisbane. He didn't get enough marks for uni, but ended up working for his uncle's transport company in Queensland. Wayne knew all about it from his Mum.

'He'll be running the company by the age of thirty,' she'd said, 'and this fiancée of his is from old Queensland money, a good looking girl too. They'll have beautiful children those two. Bruce's always been a very good looking boy.'

Wayne had let her go on about it the way she always did. It meant she wouldn't be asking him questions, and that was fine with him.

Annabelle was wrapped against the cold when she arrived. They'd built a bonfire in the clearing between the kitchen block and the water. She saw Wayne straight away, nodded to him amid Janelle's sparring session with the boys.

When she took her bags up to the accommodation block, Janelle announced with great authority: 'She's called off her wedding. I heard he was the violent type.' A murmur went around until someone shooshed them all because Annabelle was coming back to the fireside.

'How about we play spotlight, for old time's sake?' one guy yelled.

'Naa, don't be stupid,' Bruce said, his words landing with such authority, before handing out more beers from his huge esky which came with his new four-wheel drive. Someone else arrived with stacks of pizzas from the town over the hill, and they were passed around. Music went on. The hits that were top of the charts the month they'd all left school. Wayne found himself passed a pizza box with one slice left in it, by Annabelle.

'So you been snapped up yet?' she asked.

'Naa. Too busy with exams,' he shoved pizza in his mouth to let her talk.

'Gimme a little kiss,' she said, leaning up to him. He wiped his mouth, laughing and pulling a face.

'You're still funny,' she said, 'lovely and funny.' They pecked.

They talked, like there was no one else there. It was a quiet night, quieter than most imagined. The edge was being taken off their youth, and some went to bed early. One of the formerly cool girls was pregnant and her partner led her gently up the hill. 'Not married,' Janelle announced quietly as they disappeared.

Wayne and Annabelle were the last ones by the fire. He couldn't bring himself to suggest anything, just put an arm silently around her, which she accepted for its warmth and honesty.

'Where's your room?' she whispered, eyes on the fire.

'On the left corridor, as per bloody usual.'

'Not in the girls' wing this time, with little poofy pants?'

'Nope,' he said, like a full stop.

'Turns out he is a poof after all, you know. I heard he left home, left school and everything. Works in fashion. Got black fingernails and all these earrings in his face now. Sad.'

'Why?' Wayne said, testing.

'Well, it's not normal, but he bought it on himself I suppose. He didn't have to go that way. It's not like he's totally ugly or anything.'

'I suppose, but you gotta feel sorry for him too.'

'You're nice, you know that?' she said, looking past the glow of the fire into his eyes.

AFTER that, he met her every week for lunch at her uni union. Soon, he started collecting her from her college for a date.

They went to the movies. They cuddled in her room. She always stopped him doing any more, although they'd started feeling each other's groins. He'd made her wet down there, and she'd bitten his ear.

'Must be a girl,' Mum said, relieved, when he stopped coming home every weekend. 'I'll tell your father. City girl, I suppose?'

'Nope,' he said, 'Annabelle Taylor.'

The next weekend he took her up Centrepoint, to the revolving restaurant, spent all his student allowance on a three-course meal and asked her to marry him over dessert.

When Mum found out, she looked him in the eye for the first time in many, many years, and saw that her son was indeed more handsome that his father had been at the same age.

Wayne asked Dad for a loan to buy a ring, and Dad spoke more than one sentence to him when he said he could have the money, and that he knew just the place to buy it. 'Take you there myself,' he said.

MUM had enthusiastically arranged to go out for family dinner with the Taylors, but Annabelle was annoyed.

'You should have asked me first,' she told Wayne, 'it's not that easy. Dad lives in Perth now.'

'He working there?' Wayne asked, watching the glint of his ring on her hand.

'No,' she was upset.

'What is it?' he asked, in the way that always opened her up. He got the whole story. Her Dad had left her mother while they were still at school. Another woman. Family didn't want anyone to know.

'Well Mum and Dad don't need to know. Can he come over for the wedding?' he said.

'He said he would, and he's not bringing *her*.'

'Well then, it's okay. Just bring your Mum to dinner with my folks and what they don't know won't hurt them.'

It started awkwardly, but Annabelle's Mum was brilliant and talked them all through it. She was interested in Wayne and what his uni was like and how his course was going, then interested in Wayne's father and where he'd grown up and nodded through his description of twenty-five years at the tax office, and then drew Wayne's mum out of herself by showing how much they had in common even though Annabelle's mum had managed an RSL club for ten years and Wayne's Mum had given up teachers' college when she married.

'Thanks for taking her on,' she whispered to Wayne as they prepared to leave.

'That's okay,' he replied, swallowing.

'No really, she was so upset this time last year. Thought she'd never find another fellow, and there you are, you've been there all along,' and then her taxi arrived and she farewelled them all with 'see you at the wedding. I'm wearing rose.'

'Oh ... I haven't begun to think,' Wayne's Mum said.

'Anything other than white,' Annabelle's Mum quipped.

'Of course, yes,' Wayne's Mum said, looking as though she was thinking *what an odd woman*.

At the suit fitting Mum had arranged for them, Dad was awkward and Wayne put it down to his father's shock of his waist size increasing since his own marriage, but the truth came after the fittings while they were in the lift alone on the way out of the department store.

'You might like to consider this,' he mumbled, passing over a leaflet.

It read *Preparing for Marriage – an essential guide for Christians*. Wayne gave an involuntary laugh.

'Your mother wanted me to make sure you're as ready as you can be. Marriage is ... well it's something you've got to prepare for. There are certain things about it, you know, in the bedroom, which you need to know so you can fulfill your duties as a man.'

'Okay Dad,' Wayne said, slipping the brochure into his pocket.

'So I can tell your mother you'll do it?' his father looked straight ahead. Wayne nodded.

On the train he read it properly. There was Bill Timmins on the back cover, still with his beard, smiling whitely from a framed box which spoke of his 'wide experience in counselling young people and married couples in the art of walking with God in your marriage.'

There were one-day or weekend courses. The weekends were at the church camp.

That night it took him by surprise, lying awake and thinking about Bill teaching him, naked, in the bunk bed. He'd seen where men put everything, and Bill put it into him. He wanted Bill on top of him, pinning him to the bed.

The next morning, he threw the brochure in the common room bin and tried to forget about it by calling Annabelle and making a date for Friday night. She said six o'clock, not five. She was having her trial run for her hairdo.

After tutorials, he saw the brochure sticking out of the bin and called to find out if they could go that weekend. It wasn't Bill who answered but a whiney-sounding woman from the church office. She booked them in and said to arrive by lunchtime Saturday.

ANNABELLE was under the hairdryer, annoyed but placated by a large glossy magazine. He pecked her on the cheek and felt the hot dry rush coming down the side of her face. The hairdressers were busy on others upstairs.

'I fell asleep,' he said, 'just fell asleep.'

'Doesn't matter anyway, it's going to be at least another hour. You may as well go because it's just boring for men,' she said, not looking up from the pages.

'I'll stay, my love,' he said, already using his parents' language.

'The main one's gay, and I think the other one is too,' she whispered, indicating upstairs with her eyes. There was a lot of high-pitched laughter coming from up there, and disco music.

'Oh yeah?' Wayne said, not sure where to go with that. He looked at his fiancée. She was closed to him right now. She'd been like that a few times before. He couldn't budge her.

'Be down in a minute *Annalise*,' a guy called from upstairs, 'you feeling nice and hot?'

'Yes,' she called, not correcting him.

'Oh, hello,' the guy said. He was blonde-tipped in a white jacket, 'you the lucky man?'

Wayne nodded.

'Have a seat. Help yourself to a coffee out the back if you like. We were going to have wine but my glamorous assistant forgot to get some in her lunch break, *didn't she?*'

There were higher-pitched protestations as the blonde guy descended the black spiral staircase and jumped to the hairdryer, lifting it off Annabelle, and primping the arrangement of curlers.

'I think that's enough for now. Coffee?' and he looked Wayne in the eye, a watery look upwards, making Wayne feel how wonderfully tall he was.

Wayne just said, 'I'll leave you to it. See you tomorrow.'

'Okay,' Annabelle said, still locked. Wayne leaned in for a peck which she allowed.

The blonde guy shrugged and opened his eyes wide. 'Derek!' he shouted upstairs, 'I think a wine is called for. Be a dear and pop out would you?'

There was a negative sound from upstairs.

Wayne said: 'I'll go. Where's the bottlo?'

'Oh?' the blonde said, 'left out the door, then left again and into the pub on the corner.' He drew a note from the register and shuffled Wayne out. 'I should lock up,' he said, 'you don't know the trash that'll come sniffing around an open bottle of wine in this area.'

Wayne nodded, and disappeared.

It was already dark and commuters were making their way home down the side streets. There was a sex shop with flashing lights and a tempting stairwell, and then the crowded bar with people spilling out onto the street. He had to push through to the bottle shop counter.

A big guy with a moustache served him. He forgot to ask what kind of wine he should get, so he got champagne. Annabelle liked champagne. On the television screen was footage of Madonna and some dancers. Men moved in the crowd. Wayne got his change and got out.

'Perfect,' Derek said, ripping the foil off and wrenching the cork with a muscular tug, then deftly pouring five flutes of it. 'Come and get it,' he called upstairs to the other client.

Annabelle was being tugged by the blonde, who'd apologised for not introducing himself before. 'Timothy's the name,' he said, 'boring as bat shit,' which made Wayne laugh.

Annabelle was getting increasingly agitated. Timothy clocked it straight away and hustled Wayne, Derek, and the other woman upstairs. 'Leave us please, to work the magic!'

Upstairs were three more hairdressing stations and a bank of sinks. The other woman fixed her hair in the mirror and sipped champagne. 'When's the big day?' she asked.

'Three weeks,' Wayne said, arms crossed.

'Mmmmm,' Derek said, 'you're both very young. It's cute.'

'Wish I'd married young,' the woman said, standing up from the mirror. Wayne noticed her hands then. Veiny. She was tall. 'Tell us how you met, go on.'

He did, and they listened intently, until Timothy called them down to see Annabelle's riotous hair. 'She doesn't want it so high on the day,' Timothy announced, 'but this is the general thing she wants.'

Annabelle nodded, but her eyes were on the floor.

Outside, Wayne whispered: 'Why'd you go here?'

'They've got a good price for weddings,' she whined, 'get me a taxi.'

Timothy, Derek, and the woman watched them through the glass, and they all waved.

As the taxi pulled in, Wayne was sure he saw the strange woman mouthing: 'I give them six months,' before they all laughed and Timothy pulled the shutter down.

EVERYTHING went off without a hitch. Wayne's Mum wore lemon. Annabelle's Mum wore a deep blue. Her Dad came over from Perth and gave his daughter away without bringing his girlfriend. No one that knew could tell he and his wife were not still together. He was on the five o'clock plane back across the country after the happy couple had cut the cake and danced awkwardly in front of their guests.

The bridal party's hair was done by someone Janelle had used. Everyone commented on the tone of the day. 'Special', 'lovely', 'touching' and 'heartfelt' were some of the words used. There was a gang from school all dressed up. Bruce and his wife flew down from Brisbane and Bruce clapped Wayne appropriately on the back every time they spoke.

'Sorry I missed your bucks' night,' Bruce said.

'No worries mate,' Wayne answered. He hadn't had one.

They had photos on the church steps and a vintage car to get to the sports club reception.

Wayne's cousins came. He hadn't seen them since they were very young.

'Something for you lot to aspire to,' Aunty Joan said to them all. 'Well done love,' she said, kissing Wayne on the cheek and going to congratulate his father, her brother, who huffed at her and couldn't wait till she stopped fussing.

The speeches were all hilarious. Wayne made apt jokes about not having any friends good looking enough to be his best man. Everyone laughed. His mother didn't, she'd said: 'It's a shame you didn't ask one of your mates from school.'

Annabelle's father had paid for a week in Cairns in lieu of any of the wedding costs. He gave Wayne the tickets before his cab for the airport arrived. 'Have fun,' he said, not hinting at any further wisdom for his new son-in-law.

They left for the airport hotel by eight. Annabelle's hairdo was falling out so she ripped the rest of it apart in the taxi, and pulled her husband to her.

'I am going to give you a tongue lashing tonight,' she growled, a bit tipsy.

They were shown up to their room. Annabelle pulled him to her, by the bed, and kissed him more deeply than ever. She wrenched off his jacket, ripped at his cummerbund, and had his pants down around his ankles before he could get anything up.

She held her dress and petticoats aside, waiting for him to rip off her panties. Thinking the silence meant something dark and sexual, she waited, the folds of fabric pulsating in the half light.

'What's wrong?' she moaned.

Hers

ANNABELLE FELT IT first at a netball match.

One of the male teachers from the other school was the referee. He knew the rules of netball better than any female PE teacher she'd ever come across, but it was the way he used his arms that caught her eye. He focussed on the game intently, gesticulated decisions and was very sure of himself.

She hadn't seen that before, and really only noticed when she was at home later and saw her father slink around after being home late again.

He was unsure. Closed. The netball referee wasn't. She dreamed of him often, his fit legs and tiny shorts also a source of intrigue, but all that lay far behind the wonderful sense of decision making and the ease of the man.

Jesus also made his way into her dreams.

There was a picture of him on the Sunday School wall, dressed in white with sandals, long hair and a beard. He was preaching to a crowd and his hands were raised, capable and soft.

When she thought of Jesus in the same way she thought of the netball referee, Annabelle didn't tell anyone about it. She knew already that would cause problems.

The first time a boy touched her, he didn't even know it. It was when there was a group of them getting onto the bus for church camp. Her mother dropped her early so she had to wait the longest, chatting with the sympathetic bus driver until the others started to arrive in dribs and drabs.

They were putting luggage into the side of the bus, through the big doors which lifted up, and a boy called Wayne passed a bag across her chest. His hands brushed against her nipples, and she had the oddest sensation. She looked to see if he was watching, but he shoved the bag in and ran for the door to get a seat up the back. On the trip she sought him out but he made no indication of even knowing her.

He was tall already, with brown skin. He didn't take over games like the other boys, or push littler kids around, and he had a pleasant laugh.

One year she was friends with an awkward girl called Claire who told stories about kissing. She'd seen her sister and a boy kissing, and she called it 'kissy-kissy' and they all kept saying it until Joanne the counsellor told them they'd be put on washing up duty for every time she heard them say it, which meant they stopped saying it with her around, and kept it up with the smaller kids who begged them to say what it meant.

Claire said it was sex, and you could make a baby if you did it and didn't go to a doctor afterwards, and you'd have to go to another school. All apparently from her older sisters, this information, but Annabelle didn't believe her.

They had hygiene classes at camp, after Joanne asked them if their mothers had told them of feminine hygiene yet.

Any girl who said no was sent on a bushwalk up to the lookout. Annabelle lied and said her mother had told her, so she was included in the group of older girls who met after lunch in the common room.

'Now,' Joanne said, looking them all in the eye one by one, 'we need to talk about boy rules. You've all got to set a good example and make sure you don't get into any trouble with the boys. I think you all know what I am saying, but if you have any questions, I want you to come and ask me later on, and we can go through it all so that no one's in any doubt.'

The girls all looked at each other with a mix of excitement and fear, some with a haughty, closed look. Annabelle was intrigued. She watched Joanne pass around a little brochure, noticing the way the older woman flattened down her top every time she'd finished moving. The brochure read: *A young girl's guide to a loving God.*

'We're going to make our way through this today girls. No use getting embarrassed, we've just got to get it done and not muck around, alright?'

They prayed. Annabelle looked at the picture on the cover. A girl was framed by a rainbow, with Jesus up above opening his arms to her. She wriggled in her chair and needed a glass of water. Joanne heard the creaking of the canvas and frowned mid prayer.

They watched *Top Gun* that night and at bedtime everyone was talking about almost seeing an actor's bum in the shower scene.

'I think men are ugly,' Claire asserted.

'You would,' an older girl said after lights out, 'because you're going to turn into a lesbian if you keep going the way you're going.'

No one said anything. Annabelle wanted to but couldn't get over the sound of that word.

When she got home from camp her mother had filled one of her drawers with little blue bras. The same thing had happened three years before when she'd come home to a packet of sanitary napkins with instructions.

The first day she bled, Annabelle knew what she needed to do because she'd read those instructions.

Luckily she'd been at home, but some blood got on the lounge where she'd been watching a video. She scrubbed it but it wouldn't all come out, so she put a cushion over the spot. Her mother laundered her clothes as usual. The stained panties came back vivid white and her mother never said a word.

Now and then, she'd come home from school and the supply of napkins was replenished if it was getting low. Sometimes the cushion was out of place and the little mark of dark browny red showed on the beige linen, and Annabelle would cover it again.

'Dad, listen to me,' she would say when she was trying to talk to him and he was doing something else. He'd never stop and listen, he'd just pack the car or empty Mum's shopping or wash the car.

After a few times she'd just storm off and he'd say she was having a 'teenage girl mood.' The first camp after she gave up trying to talk to her father, she decided she'd spend time cornering boys.

She started with Simon, a foolish, red-faced youth who hung on the edge of the action but made a lot of noise.

'We don't have to listen to what you have to say,' she said to him one day when they were making a rope bridge over the river, low enough so no one else heard.

He'd been yelling across to the boys on the other side to catch another rope he'd thrown over to help, but they weren't interested.

'I know,' he said, shrugging, 'but it'll help them if they do.'

'Yeah, sure,' she said, 'and how do you know?' The look on his face was like a cat's when you kicked it. She turned on her heel and walked off to see if lunches were ready. It felt good to have had such an effect. Simon avoided her, but she'd never let him get away with anything, and after a while he knew it, so she won.

Wayne was a different story. She tried to get him to notice her but sitting with him at lunch and trying to get a seat near him when they had video nights, but he was always following Bruce around like a puppy.

She'd sorted Bruce out by always suggesting that he'd farted, and all the kids would move apart, so he kept away from her too.

One day when she and some others were smoking fags in the dunny, she caught Wayne in one of the cubicles.

She covered for him because it was big trouble if you were caught in the wrong toilets. He was easy to corner because he'd been caught out. She didn't know why, but his sheepish look made her kiss him.

DAD and Mum were fighting the morning of next year's sports carnival, trying to keep it from her by doing it upstairs, but as she ate her breakfast Annabelle heard Dad pacing.

Mum wouldn't let him escape. She followed him from one end of the house to the other until he started yelling, and then he left for work with a sharp look at his daughter on the way through to the garage.

'Bye Dad,' she yelled as he disappeared. That day she captured Wayne behind the old tuck shop and felt him up. He'd locked his knees as she did it, *like a spastic*, she thought. It made her wet.

DAD left the next year. A job in Perth was too good to pass up and the house became Mum's rules.

Mum would do the housework while she made Annabelle study for her last year exams. No horse riding, and no leadership camp that year either. Only organised parties with the snobby families from church. Wayne watched her like a hawk whenever they saw each other there.

She was stuck in the house so much she started snooping. Her mother kept a racy romance book under her desk, with love scenes in it at the pages with folded corners. It was boring after a couple of reads, but that day with Wayne's bristling leg was Annabelle's only other experience.

She took to writing her own stories, hidden in an old jigsaw puzzle box under her bed, about people in the olden days and falling in love. She pictured Wayne with fancy clothes and that red face, but none of the stories were ever finished.

When the formal was announced, her mother said she wanted to have a serious chat beforehand. It kept getting put off, and on the last day to take the money in for the tickets, Annabelle was told they would sit down that night and talk over a few rules.

Mum had dinner ready by six and asked Annabelle to set the table. Baked dinner with the works. Mollified by flavour, Annabelle was not prepared when her mother blurted: 'Right, now about boys. Don't let them into your pants, not at all, do you understand me?'

Annabelle was chewing a potato. She stopped and looked down, laughed a little.

'No, I'm serious Annabelle.' Her mother wouldn't look at her, kept on eating. 'I could lie to you and tell you about how to deal with it all, all the sexual matters of my generation, but I have come to the conclusion that I have to just come right out and tell you plainly that boys will try to get inside your pants, and you must stop them. There's no other way. You don't want a baby on your hip before you make a life for yourself. Mark my words, it'll happen if you let them anywhere near the baby places. Do you understand?'

Annabelle nodded. They finished their meal in silence, then her mother cleared the plates, softened her tone and said: 'Thank you for listening to me darling, I know it sounds extreme, but believe me, it happens. Push them away if you have to.'

She never thought her mother would be right about anything, but sure enough, Wayne tried to get into her pants only metres away from a group of parents at the formal.

In two years he hadn't evolved from his red-faced pushing and fumbling. It made her laugh, but that didn't stop him. She blurted out something she'd heard from Joanne at Bible camp, and would have repeated it louder if he'd persisted, but she wasn't prepared for the sight of him walking away from her.

School was ending and he was walking away from her.

In his car she wanted to seem aloof, and it worked, although she also wanted him red-faced again, which he wasn't. She slipped away from him because she wanted him to see her walking away from him instead.

SHE got enough marks for Communications and fell in love with Adam the first minute she laid eyes on him.

Dark and muscular, he looked as though he knew how to handle a woman.

And he did, but he was like a puppy too, eager to please behind closed doors, and confident in public. She let him into her pants by Easter of the first year, but only hands.

He was on the footy team and she'd cheer for him with the other girls, mainly country girls loyal to boys they already knew from school.

Adam would run to her at full time and lift her over the fence into his arms, and whisper: 'I'm going to marry you *sexy*,' into her ear while twirling her around.

In the bar afterwards he'd pay her more attention than his mates, walk her home to her college and jerk off over her, which was only as far as she wanted.

His fluid was sticky in her hands. No matter how they'd started, he'd always clamp her down and thrust his penis between the bed and her hands, which he pressed flat against the sheet. She looked away, preferring to see his gorgeous ecstatic face lit up only in the moment of climax, and he'd fall into her sticky arms and lay until it had dried.

Sometimes Mum would ask if she was still a virgin, and she was able to nod and roll her eyes with impunity.

By winter break he'd asked her to marry him, he'd made it a threat while thrusting underneath her hands. A soft, desperate threat that he'd be *the one to take her properly, okay?* Said in the desperation of pleasure. She nodded, and he came. After that, he said it every time, until they started telling people they were officially engaged.

ADAM came back with a diamond ring his grandmother had left him for his fiancée. It was a little wide but they'd have it adjusted. To celebrate, they ate at the local Italian place and he got a bit drunk, insisting that Annabelle sneak him into her college.

Seconds after she shut her door he had her on the edge of the bed with her pants down and her dress over her head, unwrapping her and forcing her down. She clamped her hand down over herself and felt him trying to get into her. In frustration, he stood, which allowed her to fall awkwardly onto the carpet.

'I got you the ring,' he said under his breath, 'what more do you want?'

She had no answer, just bruises on her arms, and sobs flowed out of her.

She took the ring off. He shoved it back on and kissed her. She pushed it off and him too. He pushed it on again and tried whispering to her, placing her hand on the sheet the old way. She pushed him off and threw the ring at him. It clattered against the wooden door between his shoes.

She would not explain, but being cornered was not for her. He fumbled for the ring in the dark and left.

She saw him with another girl, Fiona from Dubbo, at the footy. She was from a college on the other side of the uni. He never looked Annabelle's way again.

JANELLE called about the school reunion. 'Did my mother tell you to?' Annabelle asked.

'Well, yes, to be honest, but I needed your number,' Janelle replied. It was honest enough, so she opened up to the other girl, agreed to lunch and a catch up, and said she could borrow her Mum's car to drive out to the Bible camp.

Halfway there, Annabelle pulled up at a bottle shop and thought about turning around and heading back to the city. Out here it was so dark. She'd have to explain it to Mum, so she just got two wines and kept going.

She saw Wayne first, even though it was from a distance. His hair lit up by the welcoming light of the fire. Annabelle steeled herself for the greetings and made ready for the jocular, successful energy she'd have to muster. Janelle would have told, she guessed, and some of them might have heard about the engagement, but *fuck it, what did they know?*

Wayne seemed more relaxed than ever. He must have lost that red faced energy on some other girl. She sat by him and didn't need to move all night.

SHE said yes to his visits after that, and to dates, and because she'd seen Janelle so happy at the reunion, she said yes to him when he asked her to marry him at the top of Centrepoint Tower.

The tables nearby gave them a gentle round of applause when the waiter brought champagne and made the announcement. She got a complimentary red rose.

While Wayne was in the toilet, the restaurant revolved past the ocean, a deep black vacuum in the vastness. It was raining outside and for a minute Annabelle was lost out there, only the sound of rain against the window kept her in herself. *Why not marry*, she thought?

Mum was pleased, she thought he was a nice boy. 'Engineers earn good money,' she also said, calling the sister and cousins. 'They're going to rent a little place halfway between their universities. No use buying in the city. They'll have to wait and see where he gets a job, of course.'

Dad told her on the phone he'd pay her rent for another year, and that was it. 'Oh, and congrats darling,' he said. 'I'll be there, just me,' and he rang off.

The weekend Annabelle came home for a dress fitting, she found a copy of *Everywoman* under her pillow as she got into bed.

She rolled her eyes, but started reading it anyway.

Probably Mum's own copy, she thought. She'd wait until Mum said something first.

'How awful,' Janelle said when Annabelle told her about the hairdresser fiasco. They laughed. 'I always wondered if anyone else in our form, apart from Shawn, would turn out to be gay,' Janelle added 'but I can't think of anyone, can you?'

'Not really,' Annabelle said. Janelle knew someone to do the hair who was bound to be available.

ON the drive to the camp she got glimpses of their life together. Wayne driving in silence, confidently taking the road in his stride, giving her little glances and letting her lean over for a kiss. She would put her feet up on the dash for a sleep and feel him reaching out to pat her gently on the side of her leg.

They had tea and scones at a cute little weatherboard roadhouse once they reached the country. The lady behind the counter clocked the engagement ring and read the situation, encouraging them into the lacy bower that was her window seat, with the best view of the lake and the pastures beyond.

They were the last to arrive but the first to unpack and meet in the common room, which is what the welcome sheet said, placed on every bed.

Wayne disappeared up towards the block below the toilets where she'd first kissed him. She watched him a moment, greeting another guy in that stilted way men did. She was three or four doors down from a room she'd shared with Janelle their first year. Only the bottom bunk was made up. The top was just a bare mattress partially covered with a thin plastic sheet pinned at each corner with pink safety pins.

The note said to bring your Bible to the common room, and a new red-bound Bible was on the bedside table. She ran her hands over the blood-coloured surface, sniffed the new smells of it, fingered the paper so light that entire sections stuck together and seemed impenetrable to her touch.

Wayne was already there, red book in his hands. He smiled and made her a coffee. A blonde woman came in and chatted, but Annabelle couldn't remember if she'd said her name was Lisa or Ilsa, she'd said it so softly. She wore a blue turtleneck which made her face look very pink. She only relaxed when a pudgy guy called Andy came in, laughing before he'd even met any of them.

Then Bill Timmins came from the kitchen greeting them loudly and standing in the door frame while he beckoned to the others still coming along the corridor.

'We have three couples,' Bill announced, smiling with whiter-than-white teeth and just a hint of grey in his beard. 'We'll have to do some doubling up in the role plays, but it always works out in the end, doesn't it eh? Let's pray. Welcome, have a seat and we'll get going after we just ask God in.'

The whole time Annabelle couldn't take her eyes off him. The brazen way he made no excuses for himself. It was obvious now she looked, all these years later, at the same kind of man as her netball teacher, even the same kind of ageless body.

She noticed Wayne was also not praying, but looking at Bill too. The older man was rampant in his prayer, face up but eyes clamped shut invoking great learning and insight for them all, 'here at the start of these young folks' courageous journey together along the pathway of matrimony in the sight of God.' Annabelle was on the verge of laughter.

They had a quick introduction to what they'd be going over in each session. The women's advisor was running a little late but she'd be there to co-ordinate the women's session at three. Then lunch was announced by a small old woman who rolled up the servery door with a rattle.

'Can you believe it's him?' Annabelle hissed to her fiancé as she blew on her coffee, which was straight from the urn and far too hot.

Wayne nodded, aware others were looking and they weren't mingling.

He didn't respond until Joanne blustered in with her bags. The same counsellor from years ago. She made her apologies and was glad of a cool drink, retelling the story of her flat tyre which happened once the dirt road started.

Wayne said: 'Well there's probably more than just these two still working for the church,' when Annabelle persisted.

'Yes, but he's *gay*, remember?'

'Yeah, but do we really know that for sure?'

'He never came back, did he? Are we going to sit here and listen to him preach to us about marriage?' she ran out of breath saying it, and was silenced when Bill approached Joanne, took her in his arms, kissed her gently, took her bags and announced they'd start things up properly at two.

There was general assent and more sandwiches. Wayne moved for them, and the other guys.

JOANNE droned through the women's session but all Annabelle could see were the signs of compromise in this woman, not twice her age.

She played hard to get, like she'd always done as a child, needing to be drawn out, scared to show an ignorance of the Bible as it related to the frameworks of the sessions: 'The Modern Wife', 'The Traditions of our Mothers', and, 'The Bible for Wives and Mothers.'

Five o'clock came around eventually, and there was talk of videos after dinner. There was a stack of them on the counter by the kitchen door. Annabelle caught a glimpse of *Shadowlands* and figured it'd be used to illustrate marriage relations.

The men were nowhere to be seen, and all four women offered to help the lady in the kitchen, but she laughed them off and said it was all done, to go and freshen up, it would be on the table by six.

She tried to catch some sleep in her room but the low sun was blasting against the brick wall, trying to get through. As girls, this would have meant dragging the mattresses onto the verandah for the coolness of the concrete and the shade.

There were shouts down by the river. Through the curtain she caught a glimpse of Wayne swinging naked on the old tyre, throwing himself into the water, where Bill Timmins was splashing water on the bodies of the other men.

A STORM came across the ranges over dinner. The power went a few times but stabilised before the rain came with a rush of air. The four couples sat dazzled by florescent lights buzzing above them.

Several pastas were passed around with two salads and dry garlic bread in foil casing. The salad was completely without dressing and they crunched through it in relative silence. No beers or wine, only sparkling apple juice which made them all burp. Annabelle laughed at her burping but no one else did.

The men were all freshly showered from their muddy adventure in the waterhole.

'Heat got the better of us,' Bill announced, slicking his fringe down on the side of his head and hooking it around his ear. Annabelle noticed why his teeth were so white: it was the colour of the man's skin. Naked, he'd looked like a black man, save for his white bottom, whereas the other men were all pale.

The lights stayed on for the video and Wayne ignored the space Annabelle had left for him on the sofa next to her. They watched most of *Shadowlands* when Joanne called a break for hot chocolates, after which Annabelle noticed not one man was sitting next to his woman.

She looked for engagement rings and forgot herself for a moment when she'd ascertained hers was the best looking stone.

The rain set in again, cooling the buildings and allowing talk of bed. Annabelle went to kiss Wayne goodnight, but he avoided her and saw him look to Andy, whose partner was the insipid Helen who'd cried through *Shadowlands* after warning them all she would.

Andy looked to Peter, who looked to Bill. They were firm on no kissing. Joanne wished everyone goodnight and headed for bed.

So it was some kind of men's session agreement, the no sitting next to your fiancée, the no kissing. Annabelle rolled her eyes and followed Joanne.

The dirt courtyards between blocks had turned to mud. The gutters were waterfalls.

Her dry cell was welcoming for the first time that day, its residual warmth insanely needed now the air outside was rapidly cooling.

Annabelle showered in the small bathroom at the end of her

block, had a quick chat with Lisa, who was afraid they'd get flooded in if the river rose. Annabelle fobbed off the other woman's fear, but went back to her room with yet something more to worry about.

She was reading a novel everyone at uni was raving about but she could not get into it, so turned off the light and slipped into a few hours of deep sleep, face to the wall and knees pulled up to her chin.

WHEN she woke, the rain had stopped and frogs were making a persistent croaking from the water. She was so awake it startled her, and her throat was dry.

The air along the verandah was already warming again. Water had sloshed inwards towards the brick walls, but it had started to dry.

She tip-toed around puddles to the common room door, thinking to slip across it into the kitchen, when she spotted Joanne by the light of the television screen.

'*Remains of the Day*,' Joanne announced, almost guiltily standing up. She was still dressed in the same clothes she'd been in all day.

'Just getting some water,' Annabelle affirmed. The other woman nodded. 'Can't sleep?'

'No, I never do on these camps. Bed's too ... too wrong.'

'Sure is,' Annabelle nodded. She got the water, downed two whole glasses of it, tepid and tasting of metal.

The video started up again. Annabelle thought to sit but she resisted. There was another way out through the other side. It would mean scooting back to her room the long way, but she didn't want to sit with the other woman, the woman who'd explained the mechanics of menstruation to her so very long ago.

She slipped through the door and down the steps towards the waterhole, around the side of the building where the large iron tanks were filling up with the last of the water off the roof.

In the side of her vision she saw it but it took a few seconds to work out what it was and prepare to shoo it away, because something so rhythmic, so base, and yet so insidiously quiet could only be a wild thing of nature from the depths of the bush.

It looked like it was devouring prey in the course grass.

The slapping noise had another sound underneath it, a not-quite-suffering panting. It made her pause and take a few steps towards the water before she understood what she was witnessing: the white clenching orbs of Bill Timmin's bottom as he worked into a writhing figure below him in the shadows.

ANNABELLE didn't realise Wayne had no best man until he made his speech. For a moment, she was intensely angry. Why hadn't he arranged it for himself? She'd been busy doing just about everything else.

Then her Dad spoke and looked her in the eye and said he and her mother were intensely proud of their only daughter, and she forgot about her anger watching them kiss as he sat down. Everyone applauded and was pleased.

When Wayne sat down, she ruffled his hair and said: 'Are you looking forward to tonight?'

He nodded, and his face went red. It made her squirm. 'Just you wait,' she whispered.

She and Janelle carved up the dance floor with some young cousins in bright satin frocks. When Belinda Carlisle sang 'Heaven is a Place on Earth' nearly the whole class were on their feet. Janelle poured glass after glass of bubbly down Annabelle's throat and slurred her words together as she said: 'You're going to make a baby tonight.'

Annabelle screamed with false shock, and revelled at being the centre of attention. Daddy kissed her and said goodbye. For a moment Annabelle was alone in the foyer, then Wayne's parents walked out and his mother took her in her arms.

'I always wanted a daughter,' she said, 'and now I have you. We're so pleased. We know you've made him very happy.' Her husband just nodded.

Annabelle looked at her rings gleaming in the light, and went to find her man.

The taxi drive was a blur. People hooted when they saw all the inflated condoms on the side, and she got even more excited seeing jumbos landing at Mascot since it'd be them in the morning, off to the warmth of the north.

In a second she had Wayne to the same point she'd gotten him ten years ago, only there were more clothes to get through than sports carnivals.

He was slower than her, but she laughed and said: 'What's wrong?' when he stood and pulled up his pants.

'Nothing,' he said, disappearing into the bathroom. She stood and removed the gown, placing it on the chair by the enormous bed. She heard him pissing, then the flush. She pulled the rest of her hair out. He returned still dressed.

'Come here,' she purred. He advanced and knelt between her legs. She wrapped them around him and they kissed, making eye contact, his pupils like pins. She reached for him down there, missed it first time then found it soft. He was kissing her neck, so she let it go and lay back. Minutes later it was still the same.

'What's wrong Wayne?' she said again, a hand on his chest, holding him away.

'Nothing, my love,' he answered.

'Well...?' she held her palms out flat and stiff.

'There's plenty of time Annabelle. Come here, let me kiss my lovely wife.'

By Cairns he'd managed it, even though he went soft when she winced, and said: 'Am I hurting you?', but she kept saying: 'No, no ... just *do it*.'

One afternoon after being on the beach surrounded by young semi-naked couples, he grabbed her in their ensuite and it was the first time she really enjoyed it. He held her bathers aside while he got into her.

By the time they flew back into Sydney, he knew how to make her come, with her on her face taking long, firm thrusts. She'd roll over and look him in the eye, not noticing whether he'd ejaculated or not.

It was Janelle who noticed it first, the strange, pinched expression Annabelle assumed after she got married. Janelle put it down to morning sickness before Annabelle had the kids, then she assumed it was dieting, because Annabelle never, ever stopped looking hungry.

Acknowledgements

MANY THANKS TO writers Sarah Michell and Patsy Trench for first reading and proofreading these stories and providing helpful feedback throughout their progress.

'All the Worst Jobs' and 'A Quick Fix' were first published in narratorMAGAZINE Blue Mountains (MoshPit Publishing) in 2011.

Subsequently, these stories were rejected by every publisher, literary agent and competition I was able to get a manuscript to.

Not wanting to let them languish in the bottom desk drawer forever, I made the decision to utilise publishing skills acquired over two decades to bring them into the light myself. This ongoing process led to the creation of the High Country Books imprint.

Thanks to my husband Richard Moon, for co-creating the world in which these stories were finally able to emerge.

High Country Books is an imprint of The Makers Shed

publishing a select range of fiction and non-fiction

www.themakersshed.org

*The High Country Books logo is based on a copper and sterling-silver brooch
created by Richard Moon Wearable Silver & Silverware. The design is derived from a
eucalyptus leaf, symbolising the well-forested mountains of Australia's high-altitude regions.*